CURSTON'S

Wingless demons battered _____ _____ _____ nd claws. They were awful creatu_____ _____ _____ _____ nd long, sinuous tails that ended in spiked balls. Some tried to set fire to the thick, wooden doors, although Driskoll knew that Zendric had made the gate immune to such crude attacks. Hook-handed beasts with foot-long fangs climbed the forty-foot wall of stone that surrounded the city. They had no ropes or ladders but punched their own handholds into the vertical rock.

Driskoll gripped his mother's hand tighter. How could Curston hope to stand against such a force, especially with the Seal shattered as it was? And if the city fell, what would happen to his family? Could he find his mother and lose her again on the same day?

REVELATIONS

PART 1:
PROPHECY OF THE DRAGONS

PART 2:
THE DRAGONS REVEALED

▪ ▪ ▪ ▪ ▪

Other Books in the KNIGHTS OF THE SILVER DRAGON Series

SECRET OF THE
SPIRITKEEPER

RIDDLE IN STONE

SIGN OF THE
SHAPESHIFTER

EYE OF FORTUNE

FIGURE
IN THE FROST

DAGGER OF DOOM

THE HIDDEN DRAGON

THE SILVER SPELL

KEY TO THE
GRIFFON'S LAIR

CURSE OF THE
LOST GROVE

MYSTERY OF THE
WIZARD'S TOMB

MARK OF THE YUAN-TI

THE DRAGONS REVEALED

Revelations, Part 2

Matt Forbeck

Cover & Interior Art
Emily Fiegenschuh

MIRROR STONE

THE DRAGONS REVEALED
REVELATIONS, PART 2

Cover and interior art by Emily Fiegenschuh
Cartography by Rob Lazzaretti

First Printing: August 2006
Library of Congress Catalog Card Number: 2005935554

9 8 7 6 5 4 3 2 1

US ISBN: 0-7869-4032-8
ISBN-13: 978-0-7869-4032-5
620-95562740-001-EN

U.S., CANADA,   EUROPEAN HEADQUARTERS
ASIA, PACIFIC, & LATIN AMERICA   Hasbro UK Ltd
Wizards of the Coast, Inc.   Caswell Way
P.O. Box 707   Newport, Gwent NP9 0YH
Renton, WA 98057-0707   GREAT BRITAIN
+1-800-324-6496   Please keep this address for your records

Visit our Web site at www.mirrorstonebooks.com

For Murray, Henry, and Leo

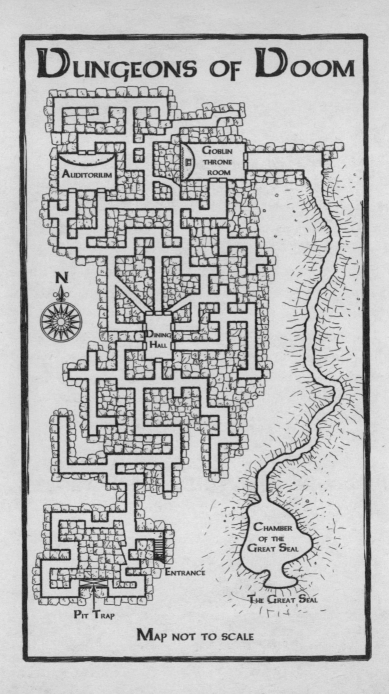

HOLD IT RIGHT THERE!

The Dragons Revealed is the second and final installment in a two-part Knights of the Silver Dragon story. It begins in *Prophecy of the Dragons*. If you haven't read *Prophecy of the Dragons*, go hunt it down and read it right now. With luck, you should be able to find it in the same place you found *The Dragons Revealed*.

If you can't find *Prophecy of the Dragons,* or if it's been a while since you read it, turn the page for a quick recap. You'd be better off scouring your local library or bookstore for a copy of the book instead, but if you must spoil the secrets of *Prophecy of the Dragons* for yourself, then read on.

Just remember, you've been warned.

WHAT HAS GONE BEFORE

In *Prophecy of the Dragons*, Zendric the wizard gathers Kellach (his apprentice), Moyra (Kellach's friend), and Driskoll (Kellach's younger brother) to join him at a meeting in Curston's Town Hall. Five years ago, Zendric put an end to an invasion of demons by patching up the Seal in the Dungeons of Doom, which lurk beneath the ruins of an ancient city within walking distance of Curston. His repair job is weakening, though, and demons are starting to break through more often than ever. To fix this, Zendric proposes to use the remains of the broken Key of Order to try to mend the Seal permanently.

Before Curston's leaders can vote on the plan, Lexos attacks. This villain—the city's former magistrate and head of the Cathedral of St. Cuthbert—betrayed Zendric and tried to kill him months ago and is now back to make sure the Seal is destroyed—and Curston along with it. He battles with Zendric and banishes him to the Abyss. Afterward, the injured Lexos escapes.

In Zendric's tower, the kids find a copy of the Prophecy of the Dragons and learn that the Key of Order is broken in three pieces. But they fail to find the three pieces before Lexos does. So they race for the Dungeons of Doom to try to cut him off before he can use the now-restored Key of Order to destroy the Seal.

Inside the Dungeons of Doom, a patrol of goblins and hobgoblins captures the kids. The hobgoblins take them before their king, who usurped the Goblin King's control. The Hobgoblin

King sentences the three to be sacrificed to the demons of the Abyss by being chained up outside the Seal.

When the kids reach the Seal, Torin and Locky show up. Latislav told Torin where the kids were, and he raced there to save them. With the trio's help, he manages to chase off the goblins and hobgoblins.

Then Lexos appears and demands the last part of the Key of Order from Torin. He tricked the kids into following him into the Dungeons of Doom and knew Torin would follow, bringing the last portion of the Key of Order with him.

Torin refuses to give up the missing part of the Key, even after Lexos threatens the kids' lives. As Lexos moves in for the first kill, Locky attacks the cleric. Lexos realizes that Locky's wings are the third part of the Key. He strips them from the dragonet and remakes the Key. Then he uses it to destroy the Seal.

A legion of demons streams forth through the sundered Seal and marches off to raze Curston to the ground. Lexos cackles in victory. But before he can kill Torin and the kids, a lightning bolt spears him, and Zendric steps in through the gate from the Abyss.

And now our story continues . . .

1

"I should have known." Lexos glowered at Zendric. "I thought an easy death was too good for you, but I should have killed you and been done with it."

Driskoll scrambled out of the tunnel that led toward the broken Seal, heading for the chamber beyond. Moyra and Kellach followed right behind him. Torin lay sprawled on the chamber floor, his hands bound tightly behind his back.

Driskoll didn't like the idea of getting any closer to Lexos, but he couldn't bring himself to move toward the Abyss, even with Zendric standing there in front of the gate. The one thing he knew for sure was that he didn't want to be caught between Zendric and Lexos as the spells began to fly.

"Please," Zendric spat at Lexos. "Go ahead and try to kill me." Zendric's face contorted into a mask of rage so hot that tendrils of smoke seemed to curl from his hair.

A cluster of shadows grew from behind Zendric, stretching

like long fingers across the tunnel's ceiling, as if to reach out and haul the wizard back into the Abyss.

Driskoll shouted out a warning, "Zendric—watch out!"

Then he heard his father let out a cheer.

The creatures that strode through the tunnel behind Zendric had no horns, tails, or wings. Instead, they wore battered suits of armor that bore the dents and scrapes of many battles, and they held war-tested weapons in their hands.

"No," Lexos whispered. Then he shouted, "No! It's not possible. You're long dead! All of you!"

Zendric stalked up the tunnel, the other figures filing in behind him.

"That's not the first mistake you've made today," Zendric said. As he spoke, he pointed his wand at Lexos, and another bolt of lightning arced out of it and ran the cleric through.

Smoke poured from Lexos's collar and sleeves. He screamed through gritted teeth, his lips pulled back in a painful skeleton's grin.

Then—just as it seemed he might have finally breathed his last breath—the cleric spat out a word and disappeared.

Zendric cursed. "He's as slippery as an oiled succubus. We'll have to move fast to have a hope of foiling his plans."

The wizard started barking orders to the people coming up behind him. Driskoll noticed that each of them bore a silver dragon of some sort, either worked into their armor or stitched into their clothing. A few of them even wore silver dragon pins identical to the one that hung on Driskoll's shirt.

One tall fellow sprinted over and sliced through Torin's bonds with a flaming sword. As the watcher got to his feet, he embraced the swordsman like a long-lost brother.

An olive-skinned woman bearing the circled cross of St. Cuthbert moved to Driskoll's side to examine his injuries.

Driskoll drew back. "Who . . . ?"

The woman stroked his forehead. "Shhh. My name is Carmia and I'm a friend of Zendric's. Let me help."

Carmia examined him for a moment, but seeing he had suffered only bruises, some still left over from that morning—it seemed like a lifetime ago—she moved on to Moyra and from there to Kellach, who sat stroking what was left of Lochinvar. Satisfied that Kellach was all right, she brought him over to the others, with his wingless dragonet curled around his shoulders.

"How are you, my friends?" the wizard said, as he helped Driskoll and Moyra to their feet. "I suspect you've had a horrible day."

Driskoll looked at Moyra and Kellach, and they all started to laugh. Zendric's massive understatement, combined with the fact that they'd avoided being either killed or tossed into the Abyss *and then* killed proved too much for them to take.

The three friends laughed until tears rolled down their cheeks, until their sides hurt, until they could no longer stand. As they rolled around on the floor, Torin walked over to stand over them and shook his head with a grin.

Kellach, Moyra, and Driskoll wiped their eyes dry and brought their breathing under control again.

"Kellach, Driskoll," Torin said, his voice painfully raw. "There's someone here who wants to see you—more than anything in the world."

Driskoll noticed someone standing behind his father, but he could not see much more than that because of Torin's broad chest. Then a woman stepped out from behind him. Although it had been five years since he'd seen her, Driskoll recognized her instantly. Her blond hair was longer and perhaps a bit grayer, and she bore more fine wrinkles around her glowing smile, but her eyes were the same bright blue as ever—the exact same shade as Kellach's.

"Mom!" Driskoll and Kellach shouted.

She gathered the boys up in her arms, holding them close in an embrace Driskoll had never thought he'd feel again. Tears streamed down his cheeks. After a minute, Jourdain pulled back and held the boys at arm's length.

"I can't believe it," she said. "Can it really be you? I'd nearly given up hope."

"It's us, Mom," Kellach said. "It's us."

"We never gave up on you," Driskoll said, as she wiped his face dry and then his brother's. "Never."

"Torin, Jourdain," Zendric said, as he came up behind them and put his hands around their shoulders. They turned halfway into his arms, and he smiled at them each in turn, even at Moyra, who poked her head through between the boys.

"I can't tell you what good it does my heart to see every member of this family back together again. That makes it even harder for me to tell you that we must leave now."

Torin nodded, serious once more. "Lexos may have disappeared, but his demon army is still on its way to Curston. If we hurry, we might be able to get back to town in time to make a difference."

"Do we have to?" Driskoll asked.

Jourdain gripped Driskoll's hand. "My darling, you must not be afraid. I did not survive five years in the Abyss and fight my way through to the other side of the Seal today just so I could lose you once more. We will do what we must to save our town, but I promise you this: You will never lose me again."

Driskoll knew that no matter what happened next—no matter how horrible this day had already been—he would always count it as one of the happiest in his life.

CHAPTER

2

Torin led the way out of the Dungeons of Doom. The man with the flaming sword, whose name turned out to be Kaisle, walked by his side. Another fighter, a bear of a man named Grax, walked right behind them, holding a longsword in each hand. The others who'd come from the Abyss fell in line after them.

Driskoll counted a half-dozen strangers in all. He thought he recognized some of them but found it hard to be sure. Five years had passed since they'd disappeared, since the Sundering of the Seal, and lots had happened since then. He wondered if any of them would know him.

Driskoll held his mother's hand tight and looked up to see her gazing down at him. He couldn't recall holding an adult's hand like this since before she'd disappeared. Torin had never been the warmest father, and he'd grown even more distant after Jourdain was gone. Kellach had sometimes held his hand

6

in those early days, but Driskoll had long since given up such childish comforts. At the moment, though, he didn't care.

Then Kellach spoke. "What happened to you?" he asked his mother.

Neither Jourdain nor Zendric responded. Instead, they looked at the stone floor stretching out in front of them as they followed Torin and the others out of the Dungeons. Kellach wouldn't give up so easily though.

"What happened to you in the Abyss?" His tone implied that he wouldn't stop asking questions until he got the answers he needed.

"That's a long story," Jourdain said. She sighed, and Driskoll squeezed her hand tighter. She glanced down at him with a smile.

"It's a long walk back to Curston," Moyra said.

Jourdain pursed her lips but said nothing.

"They're not children any more," Zendric said, his voice heavy. "They are the next generation of the Knights of the Silver Dragon." The wizened elf frowned, looking even older than his more than five hundred years. "They deserve to know what transpired."

Jourdain arched her eyebrows at this, but then cleared her throat and began to speak.

"They were the darkest of days, those that followed the Sundering of the Seal. We Knights of the Silver Dragon feared we might bear witness to the death of all within the city we then called Promise. Even then, some had started to call our

7

home The Cursed Town, or Curston, but I hoped that would never stick."

Jourdain frowned. "But things like names were the furthest from our minds in those days. We had managed to fight back the latest and largest incursion from the Abyss, and we knew we had to do one thing if we were to survive: repair the Great Seal over the interdimensional gate located here in the Dungeons of Doom.

"Zendric called a council of the Knights of the Silver Dragon and laid out his plan. He had located the Key of Order. For us to have any prayer of success, we would have to use it to re-create the ancient Seal. If it worked as the Prophecy of the Dragons suggested, it would do more than simply reseal the gate to the Abyss. It would destroy it forever.

"We battled our way through the Dungeons to the gate and put the Key in place. Zendric, Merletta, and I worked the ancient spell to activate the artifact, but something went wrong. As the magic started to work, the Key shattered. The explosion killed Merletta and injured Zendric."

Zendric's shoulders sagged at these words.

Jourdain glanced at him for a moment, and then continued, "I knew right then that there was only one thing we could do. Someone had to get on the other side of the gate so we could work the spell to reconstruct the Seal from both sides. As injured as he was, Zendric stayed to work one part of the spell on the side in the Dungeons, while I ventured into the Abyss.

"There were too many demons for me to manage alone.

A dozen Knights of the Silver Dragon joined me, battling to hold off the evil monsters of that hellish realm until Zendric and I could finish the spell."

"A dozen?" Driskoll asked. "I only counted six, including you."

Jourdain nodded. "We lost four good knights while I cast the spell. They sold their lives dearly, though, and not for naught. The spell worked, and the Seal was remade, although not as well as we had hoped.

"Despite my best efforts, there were gaps in the magic of the Seal, and creatures managed to slip through from time to time. They were mostly smaller creatures, less dangerous than the demon lords who eternally battle for supremacy in that dark, sulfurous place, but I knew that with each passage the Seal would grow that much weaker. One day, it could give way entirely again."

"That's why I called the meeting in the Town Hall this morning," Zendric said. "The cracks in the Seal had grown to the point that it would have given way soon. Something had to be done."

"Why did you wait so long?" Kellach asked. His voice was cold and distant.

Zendric hesitated for a moment. He glanced over his shoulder to see Kellach glaring at him.

"I called the meeting as soon as I was certain," Zendric said, turning back to watch where he was walking.

"You know what he meant," Moyra called from behind.

"Why didn't you go back into the Abyss five years ago? Why wait until now?"

Zendric's head slumped forward. "That was never the plan."

"You were just going to let our mom rot in there forever?" Driskoll asked.

"No," Kellach said in a low voice. "He was going to make sure the Seal held so tight she'd never get out."

Driskoll gasped and Jourdain squeezed his hand.

"You did the right thing," Jourdain said to Zendric. "You had to think of the good of the town."

"What about *our* good?" Kellach asked, striding to catch up with the wizard. "You left us without our *mother.*" He glanced around at the other Knights who'd come through the gate with Jourdain. "What about the others trapped with her? I'll bet some of them had families, friends—kids, even. You left them all there to die."

Zendric stopped cold and whirled on Kellach, his face red and his eyes flashing. "Do you think, young human, that a day goes by that I don't—" He stopped for a moment and then tried again. "What would you have had me do? Knock open the Seal and charge into the Abyss? And for what?"

"To save them!" Kellach said, stepping up to glare into the wizard's eyes. For the first time, Driskoll realized how much Kellach had grown over the past year. He stood an inch taller than Zendric now, but when he puffed himself out he seemed much taller. "Are you that much of a coward?" Kellach finished.

Zendric leaned forward and roared into Kellach's face. "I thought they were all dead!"

Kellach took a step back, his eyes as wide as twin moons. "Oh," he said. "Right."

Zendric reached toward Kellach, and for a moment Driskoll couldn't tell if the wizard wanted to hug his brother or strangle him. Instead, he let his hands fall to his sides and spoke. "I'm sorry, Kellach," he said, the anger draining from him like water through a sieve. "You can't imagine just how sorry."

3

When they emerged at last from the Dungeons of Doom, the Knights who'd been trapped in the Abyss gasped. Driskoll looked up at his mother to see her face turned toward the sun, a funny smile on her lips. She noticed him watching and reached down to hug her sons to her.

"I thought I might never enjoy another day of sunshine," Jourdain said. She clutched her boys closer. "Especially not in such fine company."

"Sadly, we don't have time for a picnic," Torin said, as he surveyed the scorched bodies in the middle of the ancient ruins where they'd emerged. "Nor the place for it."

"Your father's right." Jourdain let the boys go. "We have to move quickly to have any hope of helping our home."

At that, Moyra cleared her throat and pointed in the direction of the city, which stood hidden behind the tall trees of the forest. A tower of black smoke billowed there, flowing up into the air until it became a smudge in the mid-afternoon sky.

"I think we might be too late," Moyra said.

"It's never too late to make a difference," the man with the flaming sword said. "Let's move."

The old Knights fell back into line. They followed the old path to the main road, a wide strip of cleared land that bore the ruts of a thousand wagons. When they reached it, they turned east.

Driskoll watched his mother as they walked. Her skin was paler than Driskoll remembered it, but her smile looked just the same. He ignored the smell of brimstone that seemed embedded in her skin after so long in the Abyss. All of the old Knights stank of it. At first, it burned Driskoll's nostrils and eyes, but soon the smell overwhelmed his nose and he could not smell it—or anything else—at all.

As the line kept moving, bringing them closer to Curston, the column of black smoke grew larger. After a while, Driskoll saw that it wasn't a single column of smoke but several that blended into one another as they rose into the sky. He started to wonder not if they would get there in time, but whether there would be anything left when they did arrive.

Torin picked up the pace, and soon the sounds of battle reached Driskoll's ears. Swords clashed and clanged against one another, over and over. People screamed, and demons shrieked and bellowed.

The top of the city wall burst into view as the group

scrambled up the last rise. In the sun's waning light, Driskoll saw bat-winged creatures swooping down at the watchers on the battlements, trying to knock them from their perches. A stream of arrows loosed at the demons knocked three of them from the sky, but others flapped up to take their place.

Wingless demons battered the city's Westgate with fists and claws. They were awful creatures with hammers for hands and long, sinuous tails that ended in spiked balls. Some tried to set fire to the thick, wooden doors, although Driskoll knew Zendric had made the gate immune to such crude attacks. Hook-handed beasts with foot-long fangs climbed the forty-foot wall of stone surrounding the city. They had no ropes or ladders but punched their own handholds into the vertical rock.

Driskoll gripped his mother's hand tighter. How could Curston hope to stand against such a force, especially with the Seal shattered as it was? And if the city fell, what would happen to his family? Could he find his mother and lose her again on the same day?

"Halt!" Torin called.

The Knights stopped and gathered around Torin. When he spoke, they all fell silent and listened.

"First order of business is to get into the city," Torin said. "We can't do anyone much good out here."

"Perhaps we should wait out the initial attack," a skeleton-thin gnome with a bushy white moustache said. He'd been one of the last of the Knights to come through the gate, and he looked so nervous that his own shivering could have shook the flesh from his bones. "What's the point of throwing our lives away on a frontal assault?"

"It's easy to see how you managed to survive so long in the Abyss," Grax said. He had to be four times the size of the gnome and seemed to eclipse him as he spoke. "My blades scream for action. They will not be denied."

"There's no reason to go hunting for trouble here, Grax," Jourdain said. As beautiful as her voice was, it carried an edge that stopped the massive man cold. "Our mission has changed."

"Too true," said Carmia. "We know how to fight these creatures, but we cannot kill them all ourselves. We need to get into the city and spread our hard-won knowledge."

"And how do you propose we do that?" a dwarf said, hefting a heavy-headed warhammer before her. Driskoll had seen her working her long, blond hair into a warrior's braid as she walked. "My Gwinton is in there waiting for me, fighting for his life and the lives of those around him. Anyone who tells me we can't come to his aid straightaway will not stand any longer than those demons before my hammer."

"Are there any secret ways into the city?" Kaisle asked Torin.

The captain of the watch shook his head. "We had to plug the last one years ago. Too many monsters kept creeping in." He stared up at the Westgate. "We could circle around and try the Oldgate. It's farther away and might not have as many demons nearby, but it would cost us time."

15

"Blast it, man!" said a tall man in flowing black robes. His gray skin, coarse black hair, and piggish nose marked him as a half-orc. "We don't even have the time to debate this here. Let's go! One more charge at the gates, and death to any who stand before us."

"Well said, Kruncher." All eyes swiveled toward Zendric, who'd hardly spoken since his outburst at Kellach. "But the Westgate stands closed. If we charge up to it, we will have no place to go."

Driskoll's eyes felt like they might pop from his head when he heard the half-orc's name. He'd known a half-orc named Kruncher, a bully who'd run wild through the streets of Curston terrorizing all that were weaker than he. He'd been part of Lexos's plot to use the spiritkeeper to kill Zendric and had paid for it with his life.

The face and voice seemed too much like the younger Kruncher for it to be a coincidence. This had to be the bully Kruncher's father. Driskoll wondered if he yet knew of his son's fate?

"You're the wizard here," Kruncher said. "Use your magic. Get us in there."

Zendric held up his empty hands. "Fighting Lexos twice in one day has exhausted both me and my magic. I have little left to give." He turned toward the shivering gnome. "But I'd bet that the same isn't true of Carluzzi."

The gnome fidgeted under the group's collective stare. "What do you want me to do? I'm merely a weaver of illusions, a fashioner of fantasies. As my friends here can tell you, my talents aren't much good in a battle."

"We don't want a battle," Driskoll said. For a moment, the sound of his own voice surprised even Driskoll, but he kept talking. "Not yet. We just need to get close enough to the gate so that Dad can get the watchers to open the passdoor. Then we can slip into the city and close the door behind us."

Driskoll waited for the wailing to begin, the complaints that this would get them all killed. He looked to Kellach, expecting his brother to be the first one to poke holes in his idea.

Kellach nodded at him. "Driskoll's right," he said.

Driskoll's heart stopped in his chest. He never thought he'd hear those words from his brother's lips.

"Do you think you can manage that?" Kruncher snarled down at Carluzzi, and the nervous gnome nearly leaped out of his shoes, which Driskoll noticed were curled, pointed, and red. "Or are you exhausted as well?"

Carluzzi nodded. "I—I've been conserving my strength for just such a situation as this."

The gnome muttered something under his breath and moved his arms about him in sort of a spiral pattern that Driskoll could not follow. After a moment, Carluzzi threw his spindly arms up into the air and then brought them back down with a flourish.

"There," he said, with a half-smile, "We're invisible!"

Driskoll narrowed his eyes at the gnome. Then he glanced around at the others and even at his own hands. "Are you sure?" he asked.

The gnome staggered back as if he'd been struck. "Am I sure?" he asked. "Am I *sure*?" He threw an arm back over his face. "You might as well ask if I'm raving mad. Five years of dodging demons in the Abyss has made me anything but 'sure,' young man. I'm barely sure of my own name. I had to ask Kaisle over there three times today before it stuck."

The man with the fiery sword nodded sheepishly at the others. "I thought he was joking. He's always joking, that one."

Torin looked down at Driskoll. "We're invisible, son. Just not to one another." His tone brooked no further squabbling. "Let's move. Same formation as before, but tighten it up. I'm on point. Kruncher brings up the rear."

Torin glared at them all. "No more jokes. Stay quiet unless it's an emergency. And be sure to stick close. Anyone who gets too far from Carluzzi will become visible again, and once we get closer to the Westgate that'll be a quick way to get us all killed."

CHAPTER

4

"C arluzzi's spell won't last forever," Jourdain said even more softly, as she picked up speed, hauling the boys along, one under each arm. The Westgate stood less than a bowshot away. "We'll have to hustle to make it."

Driskoll glanced back to see Moyra falling farther behind. He glared at her, but she ignored him and watched the dwarf next to her instead. Driskoll saw that the arm holding her warhammer was shaking.

"Help her," Driskoll whispered to Moyra. She shrugged at him.

Driskoll twisted free from Jourdain and stepped back to help the dwarf hold her weapon. His mother grabbed him by the back of his collar and pulled him to her. "Where do you think you're going?"

Driskoll turned around to explain, and he saw Kellach and Jourdain glaring at him with the exact same look, through identical eyes. Before he could open his mouth, though, a strangled cry went up from behind.

Driskoll pointed back at the dwarf, who stood holding her weapon arm and whimpering. "She dropped her hammer," he said to his mother.

Jourdain glanced behind her, and her irritation transformed into panic. "By Cuthbert's cudgel, Lettie, leave it!"

Torin continue to stride ahead, either unaware or uncaring about the troubles behind. In a few more yards, he'd have pulled Carluzzi far enough ahead that Lettie would be unprotected by the spell, exposed for anyone outside of the Knights to see.

A horrifying scream tumbled down from above, and a demon crashed behind Driskoll, right where Moyra had been. The red-skinned, bat-winged creature writhed on the ground, an arrow stabbed clean through its chest. Its forked tongue flickered between its fangs as it howled in agony, and Driskoll unsheathed his sword to put it out of its misery.

Before Driskoll could strike, though, Kellach lashed out and snagged his arm. "Don't," he said. "If you attack him, you'll become visible too."

"You just grabbed me," Driskoll said, wrenching his arm free.

"You're *both* invisible," Jourdain said. "This incubus isn't."

The creature froze then, and Driskoll knew that it had heard them talking. Would it scream out for help? Did it even know what was really happening, that they were standing scant feet from him, unseen?

High above, another creature—an incubus again— screeched out, pointing down at the ground.

"Move it!" Moyra shouted.

Driskoll tore his eyes from the incubus above and saw Moyra and Lettie dashing toward him. Moyra cradled the war-hammer in one arm while she hauled the pale and trembling Lettie along behind her with the other.

"You fools!" Kaisle shouted. "You've fallen out of range and exposed yourself!"

"I had no choice," Moyra called back, pulling hard on Lettie's arm. "She went after the hammer."

Fire fell from the sky, scorching the ground before Moyra and Lettie. Moyra swerved hard to the left and brought Lettie with her, then swung back around to the right.

Driskoll felt his blood go cold. If they were invisible to the demons, that meant they were invisible to Moyra now too.

"Do something," Kellach said. "Do something!"

For a moment, Driskoll thought his brother was shouting at him. Then he realized Kellach was pleading with their mother.

Jourdain shook her arms free from Kellach. "What would you have me do?" she said harshly. "If I attack the demons, I'll expose myself as well. Lettie knew what she was doing when she went back for her hammer. She'll have to pay the price."

"You can't just let them be killed," Kellach said, his eyes wide with fear. "Moyra's visible too."

Jourdain grimaced.

Driskoll stepped forward. "All we need is a distraction. It'll help us as much as Moyra and Lettie. With all the noise we've been making, we'll be lucky if the demons don't find us too."

"It's too risky," Jourdain said. "I won't lose you boys again."

At that moment, a blazing ball of fire exploded above the city wall, about fifty yards north of the Westgate.

Kruncher charged forward and shoved Kellach, Driskoll, and Jourdain ahead of him.

"There's your distraction," he said. "Now move!"

Torin, who had come back to see what the trouble was, scooped up Carluzzi and took off toward the gate.

"By the order of the captain of the watch!" he bellowed at the top of his lungs. "Open the passgate!"

"The watchers can't see him," Driskoll said. "They'll think it's just a trick."

"Even if they could see him, they'd think it's just a trick," said Kellach. "That's why they change the password every morning. Dad sets them, so he should know it."

While they spoke, a door opened up in the middle of the right side of the gigantic, ironbound double doors that sealed the Westgate from dusk to dawn.

"Come on!" Torin shouted from the doorway, windmilling his arm at those behind him. "Move!"

Jourdain grabbed Driskoll and Kellach by their elbows and

dragged them toward their father at full speed.

Driskoll glanced back and saw Moyra tugging Lettie along after them, dodging left and right as they ran. Blasts of sulfurous fire rained down on them from the demons above, but they all fell wide of their mark.

Driskoll passed through the small door in the Westgate, rushing in after his mother, who'd pushed Kellach ahead of them.

Torin held the door open with his shoulder, reaching back toward Moyra and Lettie with one hand as he brandished his sword in the other.

When Moyra got within range, Torin snatched her arm and dragged her inside the wall. In the same instant, a pair of bat-winged demons swooped down and plucked Lettie from the ground.

Torin slammed the door shut.

"Lettie!" Moyra shouted, red-faced from running. "We can't leave her out there!"

"Unless you have wings, she's already gone," Torin said, pushing past Moyra. He looked up at the open sky beyond the shadow of the Westgate's wide stone arch. More winged demons whirled through the air above the city's houses.

"In here," Kaisle said, his flaming sword illuminating a narrow doorway set into the side of the Westgate's arch.

The Knights, both new and old, filed past the warrior into a cramped room beyond, a post for the city's watchers charged with guarding the Westgate. No watchers stood there now. All of them had gone off to defend the city, leaving the post empty.

A narrow flight of stairs set into the back of the room wound up toward the battlements atop the wall forty feet above. Sounds of battle echoed down: clashing weapons, shouted orders, and strangled screams.

"Now what?" Grax said, standing in the doorway, filling it with his bulk. "We can't just cower here and wait for them to root us out like rats in a cellar. I say we take the battle to them."

"There will be time enough for that," Torin said. "We need to assess the situation before we charge into it."

"The city is under siege, and demons are burning it to the ground," Kruncher said, looking like he wanted to crawl up the walls and ceiling of the tiny room. "What more do you need to know?"

"Torin is right," Zendric said. "As captain of the watch, he knows Curston better than anyone. We need to get him to the Watchers' Hall so he can take command."

"Captain?" Kaisle said, eying Torin.

"You've been gone a long while," Torin said. "Many things have changed."

"We're wasting time!" Grax said, slamming a hand into the door behind him. It smashed open, and the sounds Driskoll had heard coming down the stairwell streamed in through the doorway louder than ever.

No one said anything for a moment. Jourdain clutched at her son's shoulders, pulling them to her. Moyra stood alone in the far corner, chewing her bottom lip. Everyone's eyes were on Torin.

"Right," Torin said. When he spoke, he barked out orders like a born commander. Driskoll had heard this voice of his father's before and had rebelled against its authoritarian tones. To see others—grown-up, seasoned warriors—leap into action at it impressed him.

"Kaisle and Grax, take the stairs to the battlements and reinforce the watchers there. Once you get a chance, report to me at Watchers' Hall. I may need you elsewhere.

"Carmia, get to the cathedral. Latislav should have set up a hospital there. If he hasn't, make it happen. If he has, assist him with the wounded.

"Zendric, Kruncher, and Carluzzi, get to Zendric's tower. He has an assortment of wands and scrolls there. You'll need them. You must figure out a way to repair the Seal."

Kruncher started to interrupt, but Torin cut him off with a wave of his hand. "I don't care if you think it can't be done. Come up with something. Then find me."

Torin turned to Jourdain. "Take Moyra and the boys home. Once you get them settled, find me in Watchers' Hall."

"But . . ." Kellach began.

A glare from Torin shut him up. "Don't think I forgot how you disobeyed me today. We'll deal with that later. For now, please listen to your mother, at least."

Torin peered into everyone's eyes, sizing them up as he went. When he met Driskoll's gaze, he stopped for a moment, his grimace deepening. Then he reached over and grasped both Driskoll and Kellach by their shoulders, his eyes darting from one face to the other as he spoke.

"We'll survive this, boys. I don't know how, but we will."

5

I t looks much the same," Jourdain said, as she, Kellach, Moyra, and Driskoll entered what had once been her home—and now was again.

Driskoll could tell she was being charitable. In her absence, Torin had neglected the house, and Kellach and Driskoll hadn't been inclined to take up their father's slack. To Driskoll, his house wasn't a home so much as just a place to sleep. He had made Curston, the entire city itself, home instead.

Torin haunted the city's streets at all hours, stopping in to see his sons to bed and sometimes to rouse them for the day. Occasionally, they would share a meal, but food was just as likely to come from one of the stalls in Main Square as from their own kitchen.

The moment Jourdain walked into the house, though, Driskoll could feel the place start to change. He wrapped an arm around her, and she returned his embrace. Kellach walked over to the dining table and let Lochinvar slip off his arm. Moyra stomped across the main room and threw herself into one of the stuffed chairs in front of the fireplace, sending up a cloud of dust all around her.

Driskoll sat down in the chair opposite his brother. Jourdain took a seat between them and peered around the room as if it were something she remembered from a long-ago dream. "It's good to be home again."

"What happened to you, Mom?" Kellach asked. "They told us you were dead and gone."

Jourdain arched her thin, blond eyebrows at this. "Who are 'they'?"

"Everyone," said Driskoll.

Jourdain narrowed her blue eyes at him. "Did they really say I was dead?"

Driskoll pondered this. "They said you were 'gone,' at least. After a while, that became another word for dead."

"It's been five years," Moyra said, as she sauntered over to the table and took the seat across from Jourdain. "Can you blame them?"

Moyra gave Jourdain a hard look. For a moment, Driskoll wondered if Moyra thought the woman across from her wasn't his mother. After all, it wouldn't have been the first time someone had come into their lives claiming to be Jourdain. A while back, a succubus had escaped from the Abyss through the Seal and come to town posing as Jourdain. She fooled almost everyone for a while. Jourdain, however, had seemed to reach back to them from beyond the grave to help her sons. She had somehow anticipated the succubus's plot and made plans of her own to show them how to stop the creature if she wasn't around. And with Moyra's help, Kellach and Driskoll had.

This was his mother, Driskoll knew. He'd never been surer of anything in his life.

"I just wondered if everyone had given up on me," Jourdain said.

"They never did," Moyra said, cutting the boys off before they could respond. "Everyone else did. Torin did. Zendric did. I did. But not them."

Jourdain beamed at her sons. It struck Driskoll then that she looked smaller than he remembered her, but he realized that it was he who had changed, not she. He'd grown much in the past five years, while she looked much the same.

"So what happened?" Kellach asked, his voice softer this time. "Why didn't you try to come back?"

The same question had eaten at Driskoll every day for the past five years. Now, with Jourdain here, he didn't care to question his luck, but he knew that Kellach wouldn't be satisfied until he could understand.

Jourdain pursed her lips for a moment, and then bowed her head. Everyone waited for her to speak.

"It happened just as I said. The only way we could re-form the Great Seal was to have someone on each side of the gate, working the spell from both ends. Since Zendric was hurt, I went through the gate. I took the rest of the Knights with me, to fend off the demon horde until I could complete the spell. It worked as well as we could have expected.

"The only problem then was that we were trapped in the Abyss. For a while, we defended the mountaintop cave where the gate lets out, hoping that someone would come for us. It didn't take us long to figure out that it would never happen. Afterward, those of us still alive moved out and started to look for the essentials: food, water, shelter."

Jourdain raised her head to look at her sons. Her voice was raw as she spoke, but her eyes were free of tears. "We never thought we'd be there for so long. It's the Abyss, after all. It seemed death was certain. But we survived. Well, some of us did anyway.

"After we'd been there for a month, I realized that the demons weren't trying to kill us anymore. They just wanted to watch us suffer for as long as possible, and death would put an end to that. Some of them broke ranks every now and then and harassed us, but most of them just watched as we struggled on."

Jourdain pressed her lips together for a moment and held her sons' hands tighter.

"There were many nights I thought about giving up. It would have been so easy to toss myself into a nearby lava flow or hurl myself into a bottomless pit. It would have put an end to all that horrible misery.

"But then I thought about Torin. And I thought about you, my sons."

"So I fought on. I wouldn't let the others give up. I knew that someday we'd find a way out, that someone would come for us.

"Still, nothing could have surprised me more than when Zendric appeared. It seemed the magic of the Seal only kept things from coming out of the Abyss, not from going in. Lexos had found a way to force Zendric to share our fate.

"Despite how horrible this was for Zendric, it recharged the rest of us. When he told us that Lexos planned to destroy the Seal, we knew it was our chance. We headed for the mountaintop at once.

"Long before we got there, though, it was clear that we weren't the only ones aware of the mad cleric's plan. Scores of demons had converged on the mountain ahead of us, lining up near the mouth of the gate, ready to pour through it as soon as it opened. We couldn't possibly have fought them all, so instead we holed up in a hideaway nearby and waited.

"Hours later, Zendric pointed out that the army had started to move. The demons streamed into the cave and didn't come out. We gathered ourselves up and followed the creatures into the cave from a safe distance.

"When we finally made it to the gate, we saw that it stood open for the first time in five years."

Jourdain stopped for a moment to shove back her tears. "I'd almost given up hope that I'd ever be able to make it back home, back to you boys and your father. I never thought I'd see you right there on the other side of the Seal."

She reached up and tousled Driskoll's hair. "I should have known. Torin and I were always in the thick of things. I should expect no less from our sons."

She beamed across the table at Moyra. "And look at you: such a lovely young lady. Breddo and Royma must be so proud."

Moyra blushed at that but hid it behind a wide, easy grin. "'Proud' might not always be the right word."

"It's so good to be back," Jourdain said, clasping her hands together. "I just can't wait to catch up with each of you, to get to know—"

Right then, the house's front door burst open.

Jourdain shoved over the table and pulled Driskoll and Kellach behind it as Lochinvar went sailing across the room.

6

Driskoll peeked around the table's edge to see two man-sized demons stalk into the room. The tips of their leathery wings scraped the top of the doorway as they entered. They carried vicious flails spiked with what looked like monstrous teeth, and their tails snaked behind them as they walked. They smelled of brimstone, and Driskoll could feel the heat radiating from them. Their feet left scorch marks on the floor where they walked. The demons stopped only a few feet inside the house and waited. They put their noses in the air, where they twitched as if smelling something both repugnant and delicious.

Driskoll glanced at Jourdain and Kellach.

"Patience," Jourdain whispered, then licked her lips. Driskoll recognized the nervous habit. She was planning something.

Lexos pushed his way between the demons' wings to stand beside them. He looked around Driskoll's home like he owned the place, a wry smile on his fat lips.

"It's been so long since anyone bothered to invite me to dinner here," the cleric said. "But when I heard that an old friend had come back after a long absence, I just had to stop by to pay my respects."

Jourdain stood up, pushing aside the hands of Kellach and Driskoll as they tried to pull her back. She held her hands down by her sides, hidden from Lexos behind the overturned table.

"Get out," she said.

Driskoll had never heard such a hard tone in his mother's voice. There had been times as a child when she'd scolded him that he'd thought no one could have been more terrifying than she. But he'd long since learned that the world was filled with things much worse than a mother's wrath.

"Why, Jourdain," Lexos said. "Is that any way to welcome an old friend?"

"You've never been my friend," Jourdain said.

Driskoll shivered and then noticed that his mother's hands were lined with a thin layer of frost.

Lexos had the audacity to look hurt.

"I know it was you," Jourdain said. "No one else could have done it."

Lexos arched his eyebrows, impressed. "It's about time someone figured it out. I should have known you'd have been the one. There were days when I thanked Erythnul that you ended up in the Abyss instead of Zendric. It seems I was right to do so."

"I had five long years of suffering to figure it out. Only three of us had enough access to the Key of Order to harm it so that it would shatter the Seal like it did: Zendric, me, and you."

Driskoll heard some muttering from the other side of his mother's skirts. He peered around and saw Kellach saying something and twisting his hands in the strange patterns that his magic required.

"How could you be so sure it wasn't Zendric, then?" Lexos asked. "After all, it was he who cast the spell that sealed you in the Abyss, leaving you to die." The cleric stared straight into Jourdain's eyes. "Leaving your husband without a wife, your children without a mother."

"Get out. Now."

Lexos snorted, "If you come with me now, I will leave the children alone. They will be safe."

"Don't you *dare* threaten my sons."

Lexos ignored Jourdain's words. "Otherwise, I will bring this hovel down on your heads."

Moyra leaped from behind the chair where she'd been hiding, her dagger flashing before her. She plunged it into the chest of the nearest demon. It dropped its weapon to clutch at her and her blade.

Jourdain cursed in words that Driskoll had thought only his father knew. She brought her hands up and a frost-colored ray of light sprang from between them. It lanced out at the demon holding Moyra, who dangled from the end of the monster's out-stretched arm, struggling to free herself from its scorching grip.

The ray caught the demon like a rat in a lantern's beam. The creature froze. For an instant, Driskoll thought Jourdain's attack had only startled the demon or maybe paralyzed it. Then he saw the thin layer of ice forming on the creature's crimson skin, turning it as purple as a raw bruise.

Moyra kicked out at the demon with a booted foot. It caught the creature in the side, and the beast shattered into countless pieces. With the arm clutching her throat no longer attached to a shoulder, Moyra fell to the floor with a loud thump. On impact, the frozen arm shattered as well. Moyra scrambled away from it with a disgusted howl.

Lexos started to chant, but Kellach stood up and cast the spell he'd been preparing. Lexos waved his arm and the spell fizzled on the tips of Kellach's fingers. Kellach jerked his hand back as if he'd pressed it against a hot stove. Lexos cackled.

"Shut up, you old bag of wind!" Driskoll jumped up and stabbed a trembling finger at the cleric.

Lexos only laughed louder. "This city is flooded with demons that I brought here," he said. "Do you really think any of you have a—" Lexos screeched and spun around.

Lochinvar was dangling from Lexos's rear. The man staggered for the door, swinging his arms as he tried to snatch the dragonet's tail.

The second demon snarled and started toward Jourdain, swinging his flail before him. His first blow smashed the table between them into kindling. As the demon swung back his flail for a second blow, Jourdain brought her hands around and caught the creature in her icy ray. The demon's weapon arm locked up, and its flail swung down into its opposite shoulder. Like its fellow beast, the creature shattered and fell to the floor in a heap.

The chill fled from Jourdain's hands after that, the spell's magic spent. Scowling, she charged through the wreckage of the table and stomped across the demons' remains. She followed Lexos out of the house and into the middle of the street. Driskoll, Kellach, and Moyra scrambled after her.

Lexos had managed to grab Lochinvar's tail. He yanked on it, trying to dislodge the dragonet's teeth. Every time he did, he howled in agony. He gritted his own teeth so that he could give one last, strong pull, but the dragonet let go before he could.

Startled, Lexos let Lochinvar's tail slip from his hand. When he looked up to see what had caused the creature to give up its assault, he saw Jourdain coming at him, her hands crackling with electricity.

Jourdain shrieked as she unleashed her spell. It seemed as if five years' worth of fear and frustration shot out of her finger and stabbed into Lexos's heart. The flash of energy dazzled Driskoll, and he had to turn away to shield his eyes.

"You dark-hearted blackguard!" Jourdain shouted, her voice echoing down the long street. "You're going to pay for everything you did to me, to my family, to my city."

Driskoll uncovered his eyes just in time to see another discharge of electricity crawl all over Lexos's skin. He roared in agony as his muscles tensed up and refused to unclench. Wisps of smoke curled up from his clothes and hair, even his once-bushy eyebrows.

"Die!" Jourdain said. "Die! Die! *Die!*"

Driskoll stood terrified as he watched his mother. He'd never seen her so furious, and he couldn't understand how such a hot-blooded killer could be the kind and gentle mother he'd once known.

Driskoll saw something else from the corner of his eye. "Mom! Get down!"

Jourdain looked up just in time to see the three incubi bearing down on her out of the sky. At the last instant, she threw herself back toward the house and out of their way. Instead of following her, though, they reached down and plucked Lexos from the middle of the street, where he knelt crouched in a smoking heap.

Driskoll could hear the old cleric choke out a coughing laugh as the demons carried him high into the sky, one holding him under his shoulders while the others each pulled on one of Lexos's outstretched arms. Locky hung onto the hem of Lexos's robes, swinging out behind the evil cleric like the tail of a kite.

Jourdain sprinted back out into the center of the street, already spitting out the words that would cast another spell. Driskoll knew that this one would be sure to blast the cleric and his demonic friends from the sky. Before she could complete the incantation, though, the trio of demons and their half-fried payload wheeled to the left and disappeared behind Curston's skyline of ramshackle rooftops.

7

"That traitor is slicker than a greased quasit," Jourdain said

"Mom?" Driskoll said. His voice sounded smaller than he wanted it to. At that moment, he wished his words had the timbre of Torin's. At least Kellach's voice had changed. Even that would have been better.

As Jourdain turned toward him, her face softened. "It's okay," she said. "I won't let him hurt you anymore."

"How?" said Kellach, standing in the doorway.

Jourdain stared at her son as if he'd slapped her. "What?" she asked.

"How can you keep them from hurting us?" Kellach frowned. "We've blown it. Because of us, Curston is about to be destroyed."

"You don't know that," Jourdain said. "Your father and the watch and the other Knights are fighting to stop the demons."

39

"Besides," Moyra said, glaring at Kellach. "Don't you mean 'you' blew it?"

Kellach's face flushed red.

"You don't mean that," Jourdain said. Driskoll couldn't tell if he heard a hint of a threat in his mother's voice, but he couldn't rule it out either.

Moyra ignored Jourdain. "How could you miss it? Your own dragonet's wings were part of the key, and you couldn't see it. They used to hang on the wall of your father's office."

"I didn't see it either," Driskoll said, "and neither did you. We've all been in there often enough to have noticed. Besides, do you know how many silver dragon things you can find in this town?"

Moyra shook her head. "We're not the wizards, are we? We're not Zendric's apprentices."

"But I am," Kellach said, his voice dead.

"Wait a moment," Jourdain said to Moyra, her voice flashing with the anger her elder son couldn't seem to muster. "You can't blame Kellach for not stopping Lexos. He's just a boy."

"Mom," Kellach said.

"Lexos is as tricky as they come. He's fooled me, Torin, Breddo—even Zendric."

"Mom."

"There's no way anyone could expect Kellach to—"

"Mom!" Kellach stepped in front of Moyra. Jourdain stared at him, then shut her mouth.

"Yes?"

"I'm not a little boy. I'm nearly grown, and I need to take responsibility for myself."

"But, Kell—"

"But nothing," Kellach said. His voice trembled as he spoke. "I'm not much of a wizard. Nor a hero."

Kellach reached up and took the silver dragon pin from his shirt. He stared at it as he waved it in his hand. "And I'm a lousy Knight of the Silver Dragon."

He threw the pin onto the ground. It bounced three times before coming to rest in the gutter, several feet up the street.

"I quit," he said.

Jourdain reached over and grabbed Kellach by the shoulders. He turned away from her, unable to look her in the eyes. She held him tight, patting his back and stroking his hair as she whispered something into his ear.

Kellach pushed himself away. "No, Mom," he said. "I'm glad you're back, but . . ."

Kellach turned away and walked back into the house, unable to meet his mother's eyes. "Go save the city," he said. "Someone has to."

Jourdain, Moyra, and Driskoll watched Kellach close the door behind him.

"He didn't mean all that, Mom," Driskoll said. "He's just upset."

"We all are," Moyra said softly. "It's been a rotten day."

Jourdain nodded. "He's right," she said, her voice as raw as Kellach's had been. "My boys are growing into men."

She put a hand on Driskoll's shoulder. "At the least, you can take care of yourselves. Me being here just puts you in worse danger—at least until I put an end to Lexos and his plans."

Jourdain spread her arms as if they were wings, and then said something in the language of wizards. A feather dropped from her outstretched fingers and burst into flames, turning to ashes before it hit the ground. As she brought down her arms, her feet lifted from the ground, and she flew up into the air.

Moyra and Driskoll gaped up at Jourdain. She looked down at them with a determined smile.

"Take care of your brother," she called down to Driskoll. "I'll come home as soon as I can."

With that, she took off over the roofs of the city, flying in the same direction that Lexos had fled. Driskoll stared after her for a moment as she flew high into the darkening sky like a blue bird of prey.

Moyra gave Driskoll a sidelong look. "Do you ever get used to that?"

"Used to what?" Driskoll shrugged. "She's only been back for a few hours. I'm not used to anything."

As he led Moyra back into the house, he noticed a few neighbors poking their noses between the shutters on their windows. Not everyone was out fighting the demons, it seemed, or willing to come to the aid of those who were.

When they got inside, Driskoll shut the door behind them. In the distance, he heard the bells in the tower of the Cathedral of St. Cuthbert sounding the warning for the curfew. Dusk had fallen, and full darkness would be upon them soon.

Kellach sat slumped in one of the chairs near the fireplace, staring down at the cold ashes mounded there.

"Leave me alone," he said, as Driskoll sat in the chair opposite him.

"Whatever you like," Driskoll said.

Moyra stood there staring at both of the boys, her green eyes darting back and forth between them.

"You can't tell me that you two are just going to sit here," Moyra said, her hands on her hips.

"Okay," said Kellach, sulking and slouching deeper in his chair, "we won't tell you."

Driskoll stared at Kellach. He'd never heard his brother talk that way to Moyra before. It wasn't so much the words as the weary tone of his voice.

"We should have thrown *you* into the Abyss!" Moyra grabbed the arms of Kellach's chair and shouted into his face. "You've been absolutely useless since—well, most of the day!"

Kellach stared up at Moyra. "That's the point, isn't it?" he said. "I'm useless. I've been studying magic under Zendric for years, and I still can't do a thing to help. As far as Lexos is concerned, I might as well be throwing flowers at him instead of casting spells."

Moyra glared down at Kellach, screwing up her lips. Driskoll thought she might spit in his brother's face. Instead, she shoved Kellach's chair backward and darted for the door.

"Where are you going?" Driskoll asked.

"There's a city at war out there," Moyra said. "I, for one, won't just sit here and wait for it to burn down around us."

She charged out the door and slammed it behind her.

Driskoll leaped to his feet. "Come on!" he said. "We can still catch her."

When he got to the door, though, he saw Kellach still slouched in his chair. If anything, he'd sunk lower into it.

"I said, I quit," Kellach said.

"Just because you can't work your spells against the most powerful cleric Curston has ever seen?"

Kellach sealed his lips and sat in sullen silence.

"Well, Moyra couldn't cast the simplest spell if she tried, and you don't see her giving up. Doesn't Zendric always say the only way to overcome failure is to keep trying?"

Kellach sighed. "I'm quitting magic too."

Driskoll scowled. Kellach was the older one. He was supposed to be the rock, the one that Driskoll could lean on in times of trouble. Not the other way around.

"What about Locky?" Driskoll said. "Didn't you see him get carried away with Lexos?"

Kellach frowned so hard that Driskoll wondered how he kept from crying. "I never deserved him anyhow. He's a wizard's familiar, and I'm no wizard."

"That's fine," Driskoll said, not trying to hide his disgust. "But unless you're giving up on your friends too, we'd better go after Moyra."

Kellach just closed his eyes and sighed again.

"Well, I'm going to go help Moyra and Mom and Dad and the rest of Curston. Now."

With that, Driskoll ran from the house, leaving the door open behind him.

CHAPTER

8

Out in the street, Driskoll glanced both ways. He didn't see Moyra anywhere. Stars sparkled in the sky over Curston, although columns of smoke obscured them to the west and north. In the Phoenix Quarter, Driskoll didn't hear any screams or sounds of battle, but he knew the New Quarter, closer to the Westgate, must be ringing with them.

Driskoll lowered his head for a moment, and something shiny on the ground caught his eye. He reached down and scooped up Kellach's silver dragon pin. As he hefted it in his hand, he thought it seemed all too light for something laden with so much responsibility. The fact that Kellach could just toss it in the gutter like that had shocked him.

There was nothing he could do about it right now, Driskoll told himself. Maybe he could talk to Kellach once he'd cooled down.

Driskoll wondered for a moment which way Moyra might

have went. Then he headed north, toward the battle. She would never have run from a fight. As Driskoll trotted toward Main Square, he saw lights flickering behind the barred and shuttered windows. The many years of living under threats from horrible monsters whenever the sun fell had prepared the people of Curston well for this invasion. Some of them probably even felt they were safe, as long as they never left their barricaded homes, with their sealed windows and reinforced doors. They'd have to come out eventually, of course. As Torin often grumbled, most of the town's citizens couldn't think past their next meal. To them, it would be a victory simply to survive this terrifying night.

Main Square lay empty when Driskoll reached it. Many of the merchants' tents had been struck and rolled away for the night. The more permanent stands still stood, shuttered and locked against monsters and thieves, but not a light burned in any of them.

Driskoll didn't see Moyra anywhere. He thought about calling her name in the hope that she might have paused to rest here, perhaps even to wait for him, but he didn't want to notify any passing demons that he was there. Better to poke around a bit instead.

He padded toward the Great Circle, using the obelisk in the center as a guide to help him wend his way through the maze of empty stands. When he emerged into the vast open area in the center of the square, he saw dozens of lights burning along the Great Circle's edge, inscribed by means of silver inlaid throughout the cut-stone paving.

The lights mystified Driskoll. Why would anyone want to put them here? He leaned down and put his hand over one of the flames. It flickered atop a miniature version of the obelisk in the center of the Great Circle, like a candle. The flame felt cool, so he put his hand down on it to confirm his suspicion. These were everburning flames, magical lights that consumed nothing and shed no heat.

A stooped figure emerged from behind the base of the obelisk. It walked another few feet and pulled another obelisk from inside a bag then set it down along the circle's edge. In the light, Driskoll could see the figure's face. It was Zendric.

Driskoll veered from his path along the Great Circle's edge and ran straight for the wizard. Zendric stood and smiled at him.

"It's after curfew, Driskoll," the old elf said. "Should I be surprised to see you violating it?"

"I think the watch is too busy now to worry about any kids wandering around at night."

Zendric nodded, a small smirk on his face. "Too true, I fear." Then he peered behind Driskoll, his face etched with concern. "Where's Kellach? I didn't think to see you out here without him."

For a moment, Driskoll considered lying. After all, Zendric didn't have the power to discern the truth in a speaker's words. He couldn't bring himself to do it. though.

"He's at home," Driskoll said flatly. He looked down at the silver dragon pin as it gleamed in the cold light coming from the burning obelisks. "He quit."

Driskoll wondered if he needed to relay the whole story to Zendric, but the wizard's nod put those fears to rest.

"All the good ones do," Zendric said. "One can only travel the path of the wizard for so far before the doubts begin to set in: Are you clever enough to understand such mysteries? Can you apply such knowledge in a way that means anything? Can you accomplish anything with your spells that would elevate them to more than just parlor tricks? It is far easier to pick up the sword than the book."

Driskoll frowned. "He just doesn't think he's any good at it. He thinks he should be able to beat Lexos toc-to-toe."

"Ah." Zendric smiled. "Perhaps those are my fears I voiced instead of his. Still, most apprentice wizards quit at one time or another, for whatever reason. It shows that they are thinking about the consequences of their choices. Those who don't, suffer from the kind of arrogance that can only lead down dark paths."

"Like Lexos?"

Zendric raised his eyebrows. "You are more perceptive than you let on."

Driskoll blushed. He hoped the darkness would conceal the redness of his cheeks. "I came looking for Moyra," he said, eager to change the subject.

Zendric nodded and went back to placing the last few of the burning obelisks around the Great Circle's rim. "And she's been waiting for you."

Driskoll started to ask Zendric what he meant when someone

tapped him on the shoulder. He spun about, and there stood Moyra, grinning at him.

"You're getting better," she said. "You used to scream when I did that."

Driskoll snorted to mask his embarrassment. "You don't have better ways to spend your time tonight?"

Moyra shrugged. "What's the point of knowing the secrets of the city's greatest thief if you don't get to have some fun with them now and then?"

Driskoll smiled. The fact that she'd waited for him to follow meant she wasn't finished with him, at least.

"What about you, Zendric?" Moyra asked. "Don't you have more important tasks than lighting candles in Main Square?"

Something exploded off toward the Westgate, and the orange glare of fire erupted into the sky.

"Nothing is more important now than finding Lexos," Zendric said. "So far he has eluded me. He knows me and my powers too well. Still, my magical inquiries indicate that he might return to the Cathedral of St. Cuthbert tonight, so here I am."

"And the funny-looking candles?" Driskoll said. "Are they to reinforce the Great Circle?" As he peered down at the small obelisks, he saw that they screwed into little holes in the paving stones just a shade lighter than those around them. He'd never noticed the holes before, despite having walked over them thousands of times.

"Something like that," Zendric said with a mysterious smile.

"Now that I've completed the circle though—and the friend I've been waiting for hasn't arrived yet—perhaps its time to look for Lexos elsewhere."

"What friend is that?" Driskoll asked.

Zendric winked at him. "You would recognize him instantly if you saw him."

"Can we come with you?" Moyra said.

Like Moyra, Driskoll ached to be useful, to help Zendric and the older Knights in their battle against Lexos and his demonic allies. Still, the idea of hunting the cleric down seemed like madness.

Zendric rubbed his chin for a moment. "I think you'd be more useful here, if you don't mind. Lexos still might come to the cathedral. Stay here and watch for him—and for my friend. If you see either one, come find me at the Westgate."

Moyra opened her mouth to protest, but Driskoll cut her off. "We'd be happy to," he said.

"Good night, good Knights," Zendric said, as he gathered up his empty bag and strode off in the direction of his tower.

CHAPTER

9

Once Zendric had disappeared into the empty booths of the bazaar, Moyra jabbed Driskoll in the ribs with an elbow.

"Way to go," she said. "Nothing like getting stuck watching an empty church all night while the rest of the Knights battle demons."

"There are worse things," Driskoll said, as he sidled away from her. He leaned against the side of the obelisk facing the Cathedral of St. Cuthbert. From here, he could see straight over the peaked tops of the booths in the bazaar to the church, which towered over the place.

"Such as waiting for the demons to kill everyone else until they come after you like a frightened rat in a hole?" Moyra's voice sounded small.

Driskoll glanced at her. In the light from the tiny obelisks flickering all around the Great Circle, she somehow looked even younger than him.

"We'll be fine," he said. "We'll survive this. We always do."

"I'll bet that's what all those other Knights thought before the Sundering of the Seal."

Driskoll didn't say a word.

"Did you notice that not all of the old knights died or went away?" Moyra asked.

"Most of them did."

"But not all. There's still Zendric and your dad and mine, and those are just the ones we know of. There could be more, but what about those three? After they beat the demons the first time, they just gave up being Knights. They turned in their pins or threw them away, and they mostly didn't talk about it again.

"I mean, I never heard my father talk about being a Knight, and nobody ever told me about him being one. Instead, he spends his days fleecing sheep that have gathered too much wool. And your father ends up tossing him in jail. Does that sound like two fellow Knights?"

Driskoll shook his head. "After they stopped the demons, they must not have seen any reason to continue on with the Knights of the Silver Dragon. I mean, there were only three of them left."

"That's just my point," Moyra said. Driskoll thought he heard her sniffling, but when he peered closer at her, she turned away. "There were three of them, just like us, and they gave up."

"But we're just starting out. Maybe the original knights only had three members when they got their start, but they had a score or more in their ranks before they, um, ended."

"And now our new generation of Knights has already gone from three to two," Moyra said, her voice low and raw. "Maybe Kellach's right. What's the point? We couldn't stop those demons from coming through the gate, and the Seal's just standing there wide open in the Dungeons of Doom. There's nothing to stop another army of demons to come and support this one—or a dozen demonic armies. We're doomed! All of us! Doomed!"

Driskoll swiveled in front of Moyra and grabbed her by the shoulders.

"Hey, hey, hey," Driskoll said, giving Moyra's shoulders a good, solid shake. "This is a long way from over. Curston managed to defeat a demon horde once before, and they didn't have the new Knights of the Silver Dragon to help them out back then. Why, I'm surprised those demons didn't spin right back around and flee into the Abyss the moment they saw us."

Moyra stared at Driskoll as if he'd lost all grasp of reason.

He grimaced at her. "It must have been because we were paralyzed, face down in the dirt. If they'd gotten a good look at us, they'd have known better, I'm sure."

Moyra's eyes opened wide. Driskoll waited for a moment. If he'd played this wrong—if he didn't know Moyra as well as he thought he did—this could blow up in horrible and painful ways. He didn't know if he could take that. The Knights of the Silver Dragon had already lost one member tonight.

Moyra threw back her head and laughed. "You always make me feel better," she said.

Driskoll grinned.

"You two shouldn't be out alone like this at night," said a familiar voice.

Kellach entered the Great Circle from the south, emerging from the market's abandoned booths.

"We're not alone," Moyra said. "There are two of us. You're the one out by yourself."

Kellach nodded.

"What are you doing here?" Driskoll asked. "I thought you quit."

"You. . . ." Kellach let his voice trail off as he struggled to find the right words. "I may be done with the Knights, but not with you. You are my brother and my best friend." He looked at Moyra with these last words, and she looked away, still annoyed with him.

"Besides, here in the Great Circle, we're safer than anywhere else in town."

Driskoll remembered when they'd first fought against Lexos, how they'd had to go out at night and had found protection here in the circle. Demonic creatures—like the beasts that had chased them through the streets that night—could not cross its rim, and people who stayed within it were protected from them in all ways.

"You want us to just stay here until the sun comes up?" Moyra asked. "Or until the demons destroy every other part of the city?" Moyra pressed her lips together as if angry words might leap from between them before she could stop them.

Kellach gave her a wry grin, and then cast his gaze about the abandoned plaza. As he did, his brow furrowed with confusion.

"What's with all the candles?" he said. Then he raised his eyebrows. "Ah. Zendric."

Driskoll nodded. "He asked us to watch over the cathedral in case Lexos came back to it."

Kellach considered this for a moment as he stared up at the cathedral's windows. "Did he see that there's a light coming from the far end of the nave?"

Driskoll and Moyra swiveled around to see a soft glow through the stained-glass windows near the cathedral's north side. The altar stood inside there below the room in which Latislav had showed them the church's artifacts, including a part of the Key of Order, which had been fashioned into a dagger's handle.

"So," Moyra said, "what are we doing out here?"

10

If Driskoll had thought the cathedral creepy when he entered it during daylight hours, it truly frightened him at night. No light streamed in through the stained-glass windows. If not for the placement of a few everburning torches in the entrance hall, he would have been blind upon walking into the place. Inside, the few candles near the altar cast deep shadows on the distant walls. The illustrations in the windows appeared completely black, as if a monstrous child had gone through and colored over all the beautiful colors with a pot of the darkest ink.

Driskoll had thought the doors of the church would have been locked after dark, but Moyra scoffed at that notion. "The cathedral's open at all hours," she said. "Demons can't enter it. It's a haven for those in need."

"Like the Great Circle?" Driskoll asked.

"Except it works by the power of St. Cuthbert," Kellach said. "Not arcane magic."

"Wouldn't Lexos have been the cleric to bless this place?" Driskoll asked. "Maybe it's not working anymore."

"Latislav took over that duty as soon as Lexos was jailed," Kellach said, his voice falling to a whisper as they entered the nave.

They padded along the well-worn marble floor that stretched between the aisles of pews, leading toward the altar. Someone dressed in dark robes knelt there, facing them but with his head bowed low. As they neared, Driskoll realized that the candles stood between them and the praying man—not on the altar but arranged on the floor before him.

"Hold, children," the man said, as he struggled to his feet. Driskoll thought he could hear the man's joints creaking from halfway down the aisle. "Do not come closer."

Driskoll and Kellach slowed a step, but Moyra ignored the man's orders and kept walking toward him. In fact, she picked up her pace, and the two brothers had to scramble to catch up with her.

"Latislav," Moyra said, horrified. "What in the name of the gods are you doing?"

Driskoll knew that Moyra didn't care much for the cleric, but he thought she'd show him more respect in his own cathedral. Then he looked down at the floor between them and Latislav.

The five black candles standing there had been arranged in a circle with a candle at each point of a star. Indecipherable runes ran along the circle's rim, sketched out in some rust-colored liquid that seemed to glow red where the candle-light glinted on it.

The Key of Order rested in the center of the pentacle.

"Stay back!" Latislav said, his voice trembling with age, fury, and fear. "You don't know what power such wicked designs can have."

"How did that get here?" Kellach said, pointing at the Key. The listlessness he'd shown before had evaporated.

Latislav scowled. "It was Lexos, of course. I was resting in my cell when I heard noises coming from the nave. I got up and threw my old robes on and poked my nose out here to see who or what might wish to disturb my sleep. At first, I thought I'd just imagined whatever had awakened me. Then I saw Lexos.

"He stood right where you are now, his arms raised in a prayer to his war-thirsty god. When he saw me enter from behind the altar screen, he laughed. I—I've known the man for years, and I've never heard such a horrible noise from his lips, as if all the evil that had echoed in the hollowness of his soul had finally found some desperate means of escape.

"I demanded to know what he meant to do here. He said he'd already done it. He needed to put the Key of Order someplace where no one could get at it, neither demon nor man.

"'The cathedral of your pathetic god is perfect,' he said. 'The demons cannot enter here, and you cannot enter this circle. And so St. Cuthbert's powers have been twisted to my own will yet again.'"

Latislav glared at the pentacle in disgust. "This happened around dusk, and I have been trying to undo Lexos's unholy work ever since."

"And how far have you gotten?" Moyra asked.

Latislav looked at her blankly, his eyes resting in bruise-colored circles. "I—I believe I'm done."

Moyra took a step toward the Key of Order, but Kellach grabbed her arm and stopped her. She started to protest, but when she turned to scold him she saw he wasn't looking at her.

"Did you succeed?" Kellach asked Latislav.

The cleric gave Kellach a hollow shrug. "Only St. Cuthbert can say."

"And he's not talking to you these days?" Moyra asked in a scathing tone.

Latislav's face fell. "I'm afraid that Lexos's betrayal has angered the god of retribution beyond reason. His responses to my supplications are irregular at best."

Driskoll eyed the pentacle. It somehow seemed to be staring back at him, as if the circle itself formed one huge, unblinking orb. "So you don't have any idea if it's safe to enter the circle or not," he said.

Latislav shook his head.

"What happens if your prayers went unanswered?" Kellach asked.

The question surprised Driskoll. Kellach would rarely have admitted he didn't know the answer to such a question.

"Eternal damnation." Latislav's whisper sounded like the breath from a fresh-opened grave.

Driskoll looked to the others and saw them hesitate. None of them wanted to be the first to try to cross the pentacle's outer line.

"We should find Zendric," Moyra said.

"Is there time?" Kellach asked. "He might not even know what to do. He's a wizard, not a cleric. This sort of thing could be beyond him."

"What about your mother? Or Carmia? They spent the last five years in the Abyss. I'll bet they know something about demons."

"Yeah, but . . . "

"But what?" Moyra cocked her head at Kellach.

"We're knights too. Wc should handle this ourselves," he said.

"*We're* knights," Moyra said, sweeping her arms to include Driskoll and herself. "You quit, remember?"

"We don't have time to nitpick words right now," Kellach said.

Driskoll couldn't stand to listen to the two of them argue any longer. Something had to be done—right now. If they couldn't manage it themselves, it was up to him. How bad could eternal damnation be, after all? With Curston under siege from demons, it might only be a matter of days before they found themselves all trapped in the Abyss anyhow. If someone had to do something, then it might as well start with him.

"Well, if not now," Moyra said, "then—Driskoll, no!"

Moyra and Kellach had ignored Driskoll while they argued, just like usual. Latislav stood on the far side of the pentacle, unable to stop him. Moyra spotted him moving and tried to reach for him at the last second, but she couldn't get past Kellach in time.

Driskoll stuck out his foot over the pentacle's rim and let it fall forward onto the floor. Then he hauled his other foot after him, being careful not to step on the actual lines of the pentacle or the scribblings around its edge. He found himself standing inside one of the points of the pentacle's five-sided star. He held his breath and spread his arms out wide from his side and waiting for damnation—eternal or otherwise—to take him.

11

Nothing happened.

Driskoll let out his breath, and then looked back over his shoulder at Kellach and Moyra. They stared at him in horror, unsure what might be going on inside his head.

He smiled and said, "It seems safe to me."

Moyra tilted her head back and glared at the cathedral's ceiling as she suppressed a scream.

Kellach narrowed his eyes, a curious smile on his lips. "Way to go," he said softly.

Driskoll turned back to look at Latislav. The cleric still clutched at his chest as if afraid his heart might stop.

Driskoll smiled and said, "So now what do I do?"

Latislav wiped a hand across his pasty face and pointed at the key in the middle of the pentacle. "Pick it up," he said, "and bring it to me."

Driskoll leaned over and plucked the Key of Order from

where it sat in the center of the pentacle. As he did, he took care to disturb as little of the pentacle as possible. He didn't know if he was unharmed because the pentacle was powerless or just through sheer, dumb luck, but he didn't care to push his fortune any further than he already had.

The key felt warm in his hands, as if living blood beat through veins sheltered beneath its silver shell. He cradled it in his fingers for a moment, then clutched it to his chest, and stepped backward out of the pentacle.

Moyra and Kellach gathered him up in a four-armed embrace and hauled him back from the pentacle's edge. Moyra whooped as Driskoll showed them the Key, and Kellach grinned and laughed.

"Give it to me, child," Latislav said, stretching his hand out toward the key. "I will keep it safe."

Driskoll shook his head. "The time for keeping things safe is over," he said. "If Lexos went to such lengths to keep this key from everyone, that means he's afraid of what we might do with it. We have to use it, now."

Latislav frowned, his outstretched hand trembling. "And what would you suggest we do?"

"We need to get it to Zendric," Kellach said. "He and our mother can use it to remake the Great Seal."

Driskoll cocked an eyebrow at his brother. "Are you sure? It seems like there wasn't much left of it to remake."

Kellach allowed himself a faint smile. "What you see there isn't necessarily all there is of the Seal. It's just a visual-spatial representation of the arcane metaphor for the magic that separates our plane from that of the Abyss."

Moyra gave Kellach a soft kick in the leg. "Try that again, and use shorter words for the kids sitting in the back of the class."

Kellach smiled wider now, warming to the topic. "The Abyss and our world exist next to each other but on separate planes of existence, like two pieces of paper in a book. The Seal is a magical barrier, a sheet of metal placed between the two pieces of paper. But there's a hole in it in one place."

"The Dungeons of Doom," Driskoll said. Despite having been there three times, it still gave him shivers to say the place's name aloud. .

"Right. The Key of Order can be used to open the hole, as Lexos did. In the right hands, though, it can be used to fix that same hole."

"Permanently?" asked Moyra.

"Is anything permanent?" Kellach said.

"So what are we waiting for?" asked Driskoll. "Let's go find Zendric and Mom." He started for the door, and Moyra and Kellach fell into step behind him.

"Hold, children!" Latislav said. "What you propose is madness. The streets of Curston are far too dangerous to traverse at night. If they were so before the Seal was destroyed, they are trebly worse now."

Moyra shook her head. "The demons are like trouble magnets. Near them, it's dangerous, sure, but the rest of the town is quieter than I've ever seen it."

Latislav's hands trembled more now, but not because they wanted the Key. "Zendric and Jourdain are sure to be in the heart of the battle. You cannot wish to dare such dangers."

The three friends stared at the cleric for a moment. For a moment, Driskoll wished that Latislav was more like Lexos—at least when Lexos was in charge of the Cathedral of St. Cuthbert. No matter how evil Lexos had turned out to be, he'd been robust and brave, never shrinking from risks.

"Come with us," Moyra said. "If you think we need help, then help us."

"I . . . " Latislav's face fell, and his shoulders slumped in defeat.

"Come on," Driskoll said. "You're right. It's foolish to plunge into the heart of a battle against demons, but is there another way?" He hefted the Key of Order in his hands.

"If we don't reseal the gate into the Abyss, the demons will keep flooding into Curston, wave after wave. The city will be doomed. But we have the chance to stop that here, now. We have to try."

Latislav sighed as he stared at Driskoll through hooded eyes. "Very well, son. We shall try, if only because we must."

■ ■ ▮ ▮ ▮

The sky over Curston grew lighter as Moyra, Kellach, Latislav, and Driskoll approached the Westgate. For a moment, Driskoll couldn't understand this. Had the sun somehow become trapped on the western horizon, too riveted by the battle scene to allow itself to set? Or had time decided to roll backward with the arrival of the demons, seeking to find a moment before the horde of evil had arrived?

"The houses near the Westgate," Moyra said, her voice hushed, "they're burning."

The truth of those words bore out as the four grew closer to the Westgate. They spotted townspeople scurrying toward and then past them, escaping the conflagration in the heart of the battle. These people shunned them, staying to the far side of the street, too terrified to speak or to shout out a warning. They wished only to get away from their burning homes and to some semblance of safety as soon as they could.

Within a hundred yards of the Westgate, the flow of people stopped. Those who lived closer than that were either dead or had already left, Driskoll guessed. The sounds of battle rang out clearly now, and the glow of scattered fires flickered against the smoky sky.

Somewhere up ahead, a man screamed in terror. The sound cut off mid-note.

"We can still turn back, children," Latislav said. "Give me the Key. I can make sure it stays safe until morning."

Driskoll clutched the silver artifact tighter. He'd held it out before him in both hands ever since they'd left the cathedral behind. He had thought of putting it in a pocket or hiding it in his jacket but worried that it might slip out. He refused to let it leave his hands, where he at least knew it couldn't get away without him knowing about it.

"It's too late," Moyra said. Something in her voice made Driskoll stare at her. She had stopped walking and stood staring at the sky.

"Come now, child," said Latislav. "By the graces of St. Cuthbert—" The cleric cut himself off and shouted. "Duck!"

A demon—one of the incubi they'd seen before—flapped down toward them on leathery wings, his hands hanging out before him like the talons of a giant bird of prey. Driskoll knew right away what the creature with the fiery eyes was coming for: the Key sitting in his hands.

Driskoll glanced about but couldn't see a way to escape. The creature had caught them halfway down a block of houses, the windows and doors of which were all barred and sealed. If Driskoll turned to run, the incubus would run him down before he reached the nearest intersection. There was nothing to do but stand and fight.

Holding the Key in his left hand, Driskoll drew his sword with his right. By the time it cleared its scabbard, though, he knew it was too late. Driskoll spotted a pair of identical demons swooping down behind the first. Sure that he was about to die, Driskoll did the only thing he could think of. He held the Key of Order up before himself and shouted out, "Stay away!"

CHAPTER

12

A bolt of lightning speared out of the glowing haze in the sky and lanced through the demon. He screamed in pain, and his wings burst into flames. He tumbled from the sky and smashed into the pavement before Driskoll's feet. He did not move again.

The other two demons peeled off when they saw their compatriot go down. A lightning bolt cracked after them but zapped between them, missing them both.

"Zendric!" Moyra shouted, leaping with joy. "Go get 'em!"

"They will wait." The elderly elf trotted up the street toward Driskoll and the others, his wand still crackling with energy. "Are you all right?" he asked.

At that moment, a ball of fire exploded in the sky above, right between the two demons that had fled from Zendric's attack. Even with the flames far overhead, Driskoll flinched at the heat. It enveloped the incubi, and a moment later they fell burning like stars from the sky.

"Stay away from my sons!" Jourdain bellowed, as she floated down from a nearby roof, a trail of smoke leading from the explosion to her wand.

Jourdain landed on the street's cobblestones and trotted over to her sons. She took them both by a shoulder and stared at them, looking them over for injuries.

"Are you all right?" she asked. "What in the name of the gods are you—?"

Jourdain stopped short as Driskoll held up the Key of Order in his hand.

"Where did you get that?" she asked. The way she narrowed her eyes at Driskoll told him that nothing but the truth would serve him here.

"Lexos left it in an evil circle he inscribed in the cathedral floor," Kellach said, before Driskoll could open his mouth.

"So no one could get at it," Zendric said, rubbing his chin. "Did you see him?"

"Not at the cathedral," said Moyra.

"Odd." The wizard frowned.

"If no one could get at it, then how did you?" Jourdain asked Driskoll. He felt his mother's eyes burning into him.

"I—I managed to dismantle Lexos's spell," Latislav said.

Zendric nodded at the man. "You've grown in St. Cuthbert's favor since you took over the cathedral. I wouldn't have thought you able to match Lexos's powers."

Latislav blushed with humility.

Jourdain reached out and took the Key of Order from Driskoll. He surrendered it, glad to be rid of it. It may have been a device of great power, but he'd seen it do more harm than good.

"You risk much coming this close to the main battle," Zendric said, peering at the Key. "But I'd expect nothing less from the new order of the Knights of the Silver Dragon."

Moyra glared at Kellach, but neither they nor Driskoll said anything. Zendric was too busy considering the Key to notice. Jourdain glanced at her sons but kept silent on that subject.

"We need to get this to the Dungeons of Doom right away," said Jourdain, as she hefted the Key in her hand. "With luck, we should be able to use it to remake the Seal."

"Dad!" Kellach said.

Driskoll looked up to see his father trotting up the street toward them, his sword held before him. His uniform hung in tatters from his shoulders, revealing the armor beneath. It bore several long scratches too, one of which seemed to have gone all the way through his breastplate. Soot smudged his face, and he bore a cut on his left cheek. He did not seem happy.

"How many times do I have to tell you boys to stay put?" Torin started laying into Kellach and Driskoll as soon as he was within earshot. "How can your mother and I work to defend the city if we spend half our time worrying about you?"

Jourdain turned to speak with her husband. "They're not boys anymore, love. That's the first thing I noticed when I returned." She gave them a wistful smile. "They're young men."

"*Men* know how to follow orders." Torin glared at the boys.

Driskoll felt two feet tall, not like a man at all.

"When I left them, I did not tell them to stay at home," Jourdain said. "That place is no safer than any other in a city at war with the Abyss. Lexos's attack proved that."

Torin grimaced, but he did not disagree.

"And they helped Latislav recover the Key of Order." Jourdain held it up for Torin to see. He stared at it for a moment, then at Moyra and his sons.

"Good work," Torin said. Driskoll thought he heard a tone of grudging respect in his father's voice.

"Jourdain and I need to bring the Key to the Dungeons of Doom to re-form the Seal," said Zendric.

"I'm coming with you," Torin said.

"Nonsense," Jourdain said. She reached out a hand to caress his face, wiping away the blood from the cut there with her thumb. "The watch needs you here."

"Even if we succeed, the demons here will remain a threat," said Zendric. "Your work here is just as vital as ours."

"You can't go alone," Torin said. "I'll gather a detachment of watchers."

"They would just be more bodies to get in our way," said Jourdain. "We need help of a more divine nature." She looked straight at Latislav.

The man went ghost white. "But I—"

"We need a cleric," Jourdain said, "someone who can help keep the demons at bay while we work our magic."

"But Carmia has far more experience with such creatures than—"

"Carmia is dead," Zendric said flatly.

Latislav gulped the chill night air. "All right."

Jourdain reached over and kissed Kellach on the cheek, then Driskoll. As her lips touched his face, Driskoll fought the urge to throw his arms around her and beg her to stay.

Jourdain held Driskoll's face in her hands. "Don't you worry," she said. "I'll be just fine."

Driskoll knew that neither one of them believed that, but if she wanted him to go along with it, he would. He had no other choice.

Jourdain smiled at him, then pushed herself away. As she turned, she found herself in Torin's arms. He held her tight.

"I won't lose you again," Torin said.

"I won't let you."

Jourdain studied Torin's eyes for a moment. Then she pushed herself away. She held the Key of Order up before her and glanced at Zendric and Latislav. "Let's go."

Zendric walked past Driskoll, Moyra, and Kellach, giving each of them a squeeze on the shoulder. "We leave the city in your hands."

Latislav didn't look at them at all. He just hustled after Jourdain, who was already halfway down the street. Zendric came after him, almost shoving the reluctant cleric along.

Torin, Kellach, Moyra, and Driskoll watched them go—heading off in the direction of the Westgate—until they turned the corner at the end of the block and disappeared. Then Torin turned to them.

"The safest place in town for you is Watchers' Hall," he said. "I'll take you there myself."

13

S ir!" Sergeant Guffy limped up the street toward Torin and the three young Knights, his crutch working as fast as his remaining leg could—the one the werewolf hadn't taken during the battle after the first Sundering of the Seal. "They need you at the command post!"

Torin bowed his head. They hadn't gotten three blocks toward the Watchers' Hall yet. He stared at Moyra and his sons, his face filled with pain.

Driskoll could see how Torin's warring obligations tore at him. "Don't worry about us, Dad," he said. "We'll be all right."

"That's right," Moyra said, far brighter than anyone in town had any right to be. She took Guffy by the arm as he puffed up to her side, winded from charging through the city's streets. "Guffy here can get us to the hall."

Torin almost grinned with relief. "Good idea," he said. "I'll check in there as soon as I can. Stick with Guffy," he added to his sons. "For your mother and for me."

"And for Curston too," Guffy said. "They need you now, sir."

Torin nodded and then gathered his boys in a quick hug. He flashed them a smile before he left, then dashed off in the direction from which Guffy had come.

Guffy looked at the three Knights and then up the street the way they'd been heading. Driskoll followed his gaze. The winding road, dark and empty, looked long and perilous.

"It's not so bad," Guffy said as he started off toward the Watchers' Hall. Driskoll could see torches blazing from the top of its watchtower, far in the distance.

"What's that?" Moyra asked, as she and the boys trotted after the man.

Despite how winded he'd been just a minute before, the one-legged man kept a strong pace. "Being young. There's lots worse than that."

"Name one," said Kellach.

"Being old." Guffy turned and grinned at the Knights, never breaking his stride. "You'll get over being young. There's only one end to being old."

Driskoll stopped listening to the watcher when he heard the heavy stamping of a pair of feet coming at them from a nearby rooftop.

"Get down!" Driskoll said, as he hurled himself to the ground.

The creature missed Driskoll's head by inches. It rolled into a ball as it hit the street, hissing its annoyance at having missed an easy kill, and then unfurled itself to its feet.

The demon stood between the young Knights and Guffy. Driskoll could barely see it in the dim light from a nearby streetlamp.

Its black, leathery skin shimmered with a sheen of something gelatinous and red. A long, single horn curled forward from the base of its skull, leering over its head like a scorpion's tail. Its eyes glowed with a yellowish hate. Its long hands ended in thin, stretched fingers, each of which seemed to form a razor-sharp blade. These hissed against one another as the creature fanned its hands at Guffy.

The old watcher had his sword free in an instant. He slashed at the demon. The creature tried to angle itself out of the way, but the attack caught it across its chest. It squealed in pain as it staggered back. The goo that covered the demon clung to Guffy's sword like glue, boiling along its edge, eating into the blade. The old warrior snapped his wrist to remove the gunk, and it slapped into the cobblestones where it bubbled angrily.

"It's hurt!" Moyra said, pointing at the demon's leg. Not until then did Driskoll notice that a large chunk of the creature seemed to be missing. It walked with a limp as pronounced as Guffy's, but its injury was far fresher. No blood streamed from it, forcing Driskoll to wonder if such a wound would be as bad for a demon as it would be for someone like him.

The demon slashed at Guffy with its finger-blades. The

watcher parried the first hand, but the second reached in over his guard and laid open his shoulder. Guffy howled in pain and dropped his sword.

"It's a babau," Kellach said. "An acid-skinned assassin demon. It must have been watching from the rooftop, waiting for a chance to strike."

"I don't care about its name. How do we kill—?" Driskoll cut himself off as he saw Moyra dash toward the thing.

She lashed out with her foot, kicking the demon in its wound. It screeched, its knees—which bent like a dog's—buckling. As it fell backward, she snatched at its horn and yanked it.

The demon went down hard, squealing again before scrambled away from a vicious follow-up kick.

"We can't kill it," Kellach said. "It's way too powerful."

"Someone's already taken a chunk out of it," Moyra said, as she backed up to join the other Knights, out of range of the demon's claws. "We just have to finish it off."

The demon bounded to its feet and snarled.

"And how are we supposed to do that?" Kellach asked.

Driskoll drew his sword. From what little he knew about demons—mostly from Kellach showing off after a long day's studying at Zendric's tower—he felt sure his blade wouldn't be much use against it. Still, he had to try.

"Maybe we can outrun it," Driskoll said.

"Guffy can't," said Kellach.

"Can't you zap it with a spell?" Moyra asked.

Kellach growled in frustration. "It would just laugh."

The creature started to do just that, with a low chuckle that sounded something like raw bones rubbing against one another.

Driskoll groaned then, as he heard the sound of wings flapping overhead, coming in from behind. Having to face this babau was bad enough. With something else bearing down on them, what hope did they have? Fighting despair, Driskoll stepped forward and stabbed at the demon with his blade. He knew this opened him up to the attack from the creature behind him, but at least he hoped it might draw the thing's attention away from the others.

The babau batted away Driskoll's blade and snorted at his efforts. Then he looked up over the knight's head and snarled. Something small and shiny zipped through the air and smacked straight into the demon's face. It fell backward, tearing at the thing with its claws. Then its head burst into flames. The babau wailed as it ripped at its attacker. Its long fingers hurt itself more than its foe, and the flames—which seem to have started inside its fang-filled mouth—finally took their toll. The babau flung its enemy from its face, then collapsed on the cobblestones, and did not move again.

In the light of the demon's burning head, Driskoll could see just what it was that had attacked the creature.

"Locky!" Kellach cried, dashing toward his clockwork dragonet.

He started to scoop up Lochinvar in his hands, but dropped the dragonet just as fast. The babau's goo bubbled away at

Lochinvar's metallic skin, eating away at it and at Kellach's fingers too. Kellach wiped his hands on the cobblestones of the street and then tore the left sleeve from his robe. He used the fabric to wipe the dragonet clean, and then cast the scrap aside. Driskoll watched the babau's acidic secretions continue to break the sleeve down into sludge.

"Is he okay?" Moyra said. "I mean, will he be okay?"

"I—I think so," Kellach said, as he knelt over Lochinvar and examined him.

From where Driskoll stood, the little dragonet didn't look so good. His skin bore a dozens pockmarks from the demon's acid, and one of his wings had been bent back so far that Driskoll was surprised it could still be attached to his body.

"Guffy!" Moyra said, her voice filled with concern for the man and shame that they had forgotten him for a moment.

Driskoll dashed over to the fallen watcher, right behind Moyra. They each knelt next to him, one on either side.

"It's all right," Guffy said, clutching at his injured shoulder with his other hand. He spoke through clenched teeth. "I'll be fine."

"Can you get up?" Moyra asked. She and Driskoll tried to help pull the man to his foot, but they backed off when he yelped in pain.

"Just give me a minute," he said. "I'll be fine."

"I don't know if we have that long," said Kellach, holding Lochinvar up before him. "We have to go after Zendric and Mom and stop them—right now!"

Driskoll stared at his brother. "You're mad. They've got to be halfway to the Dungeons by now. Even if we wanted to, there's no way we could . . . "

Faced with what he saw, Driskoll let his voice trail off.

"What?" Guffy asked. "What is it?"

Moyra looked at Lochinvar and gasped. She'd seen what Driskoll had, what Kellach had noticed before them all.

Maybe the thrill of being saved from the demon had shut off the critical parts of Driskoll's brain. Maybe he had just been so happy to see the dragonet that he hadn't noticed this right away. Now, though, it seemed obvious. The last time Driskoll had seen Lochinvar—his jaws clamped tightly around the hem of Lexos's robe as a pair of incubi hauled him away into the sky—the dragonet had been missing one thing: his wings, the part of him that had been fashioned out of the Key of Order. The same Key that Jourdain, Zendric, and Latislav had rushed off with to the Dungeons of Doom. But now, huddled there in Kellach's arms, Lochinvar had his wings once again.

14

So your little machine there has wings," Guffy said. "Hasn't he always?"

Kellach grimaced. Driskoll could see him counting to ten in his head, trying to ease his frustration at not being able to make someone understand him. This happened more often with adults than kids, it seemed. Kids listened to Kellach. They trusted him. Adults, on the other hand, often dismissed Kellach—and Moyra and Driskoll with him. They rarely thought he could have something interesting to say, much less mortally important. Kellach had ranted about this more than once, and Driskoll knew the routine of his complaints backward and forward. It impressed him to see his brother swallow all his regular gripes right now, until he could get Guffy to listen.

"Have you ever seen the Key of Order?" Kellach said.

Guffy shook his head.

"It looks like a dragon. It even has wings like this." Kellach pointed at Locky. "In fact, Lochinvar's wings are part of the Key of Order."

Guffy frowned. "But didn't you say your mother and Zendric and Latislav were taking the Key of Order into the Dungeons?" Understanding dawned on the old watcher's face. "You mean the wings of the Key of Order are . . . "

"Fake," Kellach said flatly.

"We have to get to the Dungeons of Doom," Guffy said, his face blanching with fear.

Kellach grunted a pleased agreement.

"But how?" Driskoll said. "Isn't the Westgate sealed?"

"They'll open it for Guffy," Moyra said. "He's a sergeant of the watch."

Guffy winced. "Normally, but Torin's worried about shape-changers tricking the men at that post into opening the gate. Only he can give the order for it to be opened until dawn."

"But we can't wait that long," said Kellach. "Let's head for the gate. Maybe we'll spot Dad along the way."

The Westgate only lay a hundred yards off, but Guffy and the trio of Knights couldn't spot Torin anywhere.

"It sure is quiet here," Moyra said. "Too quiet."

"The battle moved north along the wall," Guffy said. "Knowing your father, he's right in the thick of it."

"Then that's where we need to go," Kellach said.

Guffy shook his head. "I'm not taking you young ones into the middle of a demon-infested warzone."

"But we can't just sit here and hope our father wanders by," said Kellach. "Someone has tampered with the Key of Order. We have to stop Mom and Zendric from using it."

"What's the worse that could happen?" asked Moyra, looking around a house burning nearby. "I mean, demons are rampaging through the city streets already. How much worse could it get?"

"Far worse, miss," said Guffy. The old man clutched his bloodied shoulder. "This here is nothing compared to the Sundering of the Seal. We nearly lost the whole town back then."

"If Mom and Zendric use the Key they have on the Seal, what's going to happen?" Driskoll asked.

Kellach craned his neck back to look at the top of the Westgate, which towered forty feet in the air. "I don't know. My guess is the gateway the Seal was supposed to block will grow bigger. That means that even larger demons can come into our world."

"Just how large are we talking?" asked Moyra.

Kellach jabbed his chin at the ironbound Westgate. "Powerful enough to walk through that as if it were paper."

"Maybe if we talk to the guards," Driskoll started.

"I don't think they're even there," Moyra said, peering into the tunnel that ran through the wall. "It looks like they just locked the place up and left."

"Can you pick the lock?"

"Maybe, but it'll take time."

"How about . . . ?" Kellach looked Moyra in the eyes and let the question hang in the air.

"You mean the secret thieves' paths?" Moyra said. "The ones you don't want to mention in front of a watcher—ever?"

Kellach grimaced at her.

"That's a great idea," Moyra said, her eyes sparkling. "Under any other circumstances, I wouldn't consider it, of course, but—"

"It won't work," Guffy said. "We sealed those off too."

"What?" Moyra gasped. "But how did you know?"

"Breddo told us all about them as soon as the demons showed up," Guffy said, blushing a bit. "He didn't want the buggers finding those tunnels and using them to get into the city."

Moyra blanched. "Then what are we going to do?"

"I'll get you over that wall," Guffy said, his voice little more than a low growl.

"You have the keys?" Driskoll asked. "Why didn't you say so?"

He stared as Guffy fell to the stump of his leg with a pained grunt. He started to try to help the man up, but Guffy swiped at him with his crutch before he could get close enough even to touch him.

Kellach motioned for Driskoll to keep quiet and stay back. "He didn't say he'd get us through the wall. He said 'over' it."

Guffy pitched over on his side. The sergeant writhed in the flickering light from the burning buildings nearby. At first, he looked like he might try to crawl out of his own skin. Then his skin darkened and began to move.

85

"What's happening to him?" Moyra asked. "Did that assassin demon do something to him?"

"Keep back!" Guffy growled. His voice sounded like someone had stabbed him in a dozen places at once.

Guffy's mouth and nose began to stretch out from the rest of his face, and he drew back his blackened lips to reveal jaws filled to bursting with long fangs and teeth. His eyes grew wide and filled with the slick color of ebony.

"Is that—hair?" Moyra asked.

"We should run," Driskoll said softly. He said it because he couldn't find a way to make his own legs work, but he hoped that if the others broke away he might find a way to follow them.

Before any of the young knights could make a move, Guffy cast aside his crutch and vaulted to his feet. He towered over them now—standing at least eight feet tall—and glared down at them with hunter's eyes. He tossed back his head and howled up at the moon peering down over the burning city. The yowl echoed through the Westgate.

"I wondered about that," Kellach said.

"What?" Driskoll asked, feeling himself starting to panic. "What?"

"How Guffy had avoided becoming a werewolf after losing his leg to one."

"Looks like he didn't," said Moyra, "unless maybe he got bit by a fur coat."

Guffy leaped forward and plucked her from her feet. Moyra screamed. Driskoll reached for his sword, wondering how long he could stand against such a massive and powerful beast. His best guess was not long. Before he could even clear his blade from its scabbard, though, the werewolf snatched Driskoll up as well. The werewolf growled as he flicked his head at Kellach and then his back.

"All—all right," Kellach said. He charged toward the beast and leaped up onto his shoulders from behind. With a bit of effort, he scaled the werewolf's back until he could wrap his arms around the creature's neck.

Driskoll had stopped struggling at this point. He hadn't been able to get his sword out, but that didn't seem to matter. He knew that the werewolf could have torn his throat out in a split second. If Driskoll was still alive, it was because the creature wanted him that way. Could a part of Guffy still be aware inside the beast's furry pelt?

"Let's go," Kellach said.

The werewolf juggled Moyra for a moment, then stuffed her under his other arm, right next to Driskoll. His right arm free, he crouched back on his mighty haunches for a moment, and then leaped. The next thing Driskoll knew, the werewolf was scrambling over the top of the wall protecting Curston from the wild lands beyond. Off to the right, Driskoll could see the battle raging on. Demons of all sorts—winged, scaled, burning, or worse—sought to enter the city. Those that achieved their goal swarmed past the watchers on the wall, seeking the safety of the inner city, hoping—Driskoll guessed—to spread their horror among less-brave souls.

Unseen in the distance, Torin shouted to rally his troops against the demon horde. "For Curston!" he shouted. "For Curston and for Promise!"

The beast pulled Moyra from under his right arm and placed her under his left, leaving Driskoll right where he was. The creature's tongue lolled from its lips, and it panted hard from the exertion of topping the wall. The werewolf stepped up on the top of the battlements that looked out over the darkness beyond. The light of the moon shone down on the landscape, illuminating the thin ribbon of road that ran west, between the wide swathes of forest and toward lands unknown. The creature seemed to hesitate there for a moment, although whether in fear or perhaps in some sort of respect for the lands it meant to enter, Driskoll could not know. Then the werewolf leaped out into the night air. He landed in a crouch as he hit the ground, still holding onto Moyra and Driskoll. Kellach grunted, and for a moment Driskoll feared that he'd fallen and smacked into the road on his own.

Then Kellach leaned his head around the werewolf's neck. "Are you all right?" he asked Driskoll and Moyra. They both nodded up at him.

"How about you?" he asked the werewolf. The creature bared his teeth at Kellach in what Driskoll could only guess was meant to approximate a smile.

"His leg grew back," Moyra said in awe.

The werewolf thumped down with his foot where only a stump had been minutes before. He growled.

"We need to keep moving," Kellach said.

The werewolf nodded, and they moved off into the horrible darkness, toward the Dungeons of Doom.

15

G et back, you fiends!" Latislav cried out from the wrecked square in the center of the ruins that sat over the Dungeons of Doom. "Back!"

Guffy barely took the time to put Moyra and Driskoll down before turning to face the demons. Kellach dropped to the ground just as the sergeant leaped into the fray.

During the terrifying race through the darkness, only one thought kept racing through Driskoll's head. Thank the gods Guffy was on their side. The werewolf version of the kind sergeant moved with a hunter's cold, sleek grace. Each of his long, loping strides struck true, never faltering, never swaying from the right path. When they reached the turnoff to the overgrown road that led to the ruins, Driskoll couldn't even see it, but the werewolf had raced along it like just another turn in a track.

They hadn't seen any demons along the way. It seemed as if all of them had gone to attack Curston, leaving no one to protect the gateway into the Abyss. Or so Driskoll had hoped. Once they'd reached the ruins, though, Driskoll knew that they hadn't been so lucky. The sounds of battle echoed off the crumbling walls. Driskoll had expected to come upon Jourdain, Zendric, and Latislav battling some unnamable horror in the central square there. His heart sank when he spotted the cleric, alone.

Latislav stood in the center of a circle drawn around the entrance to the stairwell into the Dungeons of Doom. A handful of demons of different types surrounded Latislav: two incubi and a trio of quasits. Alone, none of them might have stood a chance against the cleric, but together they had him crumbling to his knees in fear.

Guffy slammed into the incubi and brought them to the ground. The two had been hovering close together, and the werewolf could reach them both within his massive reach. They disappeared in a heap beneath him as Guffy brought them crashing to the ground, fur flying and wings flapping.

Latislav screamed at the sight of the werewolf. The quasits cackled at the cleric and their compatriots entangled in battle with the newcomer. Then they saw the Knights.

"The circle!" Kellach said, already dashing forward, "Run for it!"

Sometimes Driskoll questioned his brother's judgment. Things like running straight toward a group of demons, any one of which could probably have killed them all, often triggered that kind of hesitation. At that moment, though, Driskoll didn't second-guess Kellach for an instant. He just put his head down and ran right after him.

Moyra, who'd always been faster than Driskoll, passed him only a few steps along. She had even caught up with Kellach by the time he dived across the edge of the circle, and the two landed in a heap at Latislav's feet.

As soon as the quasits spotted the Knights, they had split up: one demon per Knight. The two following Kellach and Moyra stopped short of the edge of the circle when the kids crossed it, as if the circle formed some sort of invisible wall the creatures dared not touch.

The one that came after Driskoll, though, swooped right down in front of him. "Where do you think you're going, morsel?" the bat-winged cherub said with a cackle.

Driskoll didn't say a word. He knew that talking with this demon would only give the other two a chance to gang up on him. Instead, he lowered his shoulder and charged.

This surprised the demon, and he howled at Driskoll's bravado. Driskoll had never been a large boy. Having to live mostly on his brother's cooking kept him from ever eating too much. But he had many pounds on the little demon. He slammed the quasit back toward the circle.

The quasit, seeing how close the blow had driven it to the circle, pumped his wings in a blur. They carried him high above, away from the circle—and from Driskoll, who slid to a stop as he crossed into the circle's protected area.

"Cuthbert's cudgel!" Latislav said, his eyes wide with fear.

"What are you children doing here?"

Kellach pulled Lochinvar from where he'd curled up inside the apprentice's robes. The dragonet's body bore scars from the babau's acidic goo, but its wings were unharmed. Now that Driskoll got a good look at Lochinvar's back, he saw that the wings weren't damaged at all, just poorly attached.

"They're here for dinner," one of the quasits whispered from just beyond the circle's edge. "Ours!"

The werewolf howled as his fur erupted in flames. The incubi Guffy had been fighting took to the air as he leaped away from them, trying to beat out the fire.

"Over here!" Kellach yelled.

The werewolf rolled over into the circle, and the kids fell on him, trying to beat out the fire. Driskoll stripped off his jacket and used it to smother the flames around the creature's head and shoulders. Moyra did the same with her vest. Kellach chanted something quick and fierce and pointed three fingers at the rest of the flames, and they disappeared, leaving behind not even a puff of smoke.

"Stand back, children!" Latislav said, his hands crackling with magical energy. "I will finish off this horror!"

"No!" Driskoll said. He flung his scorched jacket into the cleric's face.

Latislav yelped in pain and surprise, his spell fizzling on his fingertips. After a moment's struggle, he flung the jacket away into the darkness. One of the quasits caught it in midair and set it ablaze.

"You'll pay for that, you—" Latislav cut himself off as he spied Guffy lying on the ground, Moyra holding his head in her lap. "Sergeant?" He didn't seem to believe his eyes.

"Evening," Guffy said, his tone brave, but his voice raspy. "This is a right pickle we've gotten ourselves into here, isn't it?" He struggled to one elbow. "You kids all right?"

Driskoll stared at the man. His skin bore horrible burns, and much of the hair on the top of his head was gone, including his eyebrows. His eyes watered from the constant pain.

"Help him," Moyra said to Latislav. "You're a cleric."

Latislav started to say something but choked.

"Forget that right now," Guffy said. "We haven't got the time. Get yourself down into that dungeon and find your mother. If we can't manage that, well . . . Nothing else really matters at the moment, does it?"

"But, Guffy," Driskoll started.

"Go!" the sergeant rasped. He looked helpless and cold lying there in the circle, his skin blistered, his clothes shredded, and his leg missing once again. "And take that useless excuse for a cleric with you!"

Latislav began to protest, but Kellach took him by the elbow. "Lexos tampered with the Key of Order," the apprentice said. "We have to stop Zendric and my mother from using it."

"Ah," the cleric said, glancing down at the dragonet. "We have no time to lose then. If we hurry, we might still be able to catch them, St. Cuthbert willing."

95

"What about Guffy?" Moyra said, standing over the man now.

"The circle of protection here should keep him safe until we get back," Kellach said.

"But—"

"Go!" Guffy roared, although the effort sent him into a fit of coughing. The young Knights jumped into action with his order.

"Do you think you can find the chamber again?" Kellach asked Moyra, already heading down the stairs. As he went, he snatched up a burnt-out torch. He chanted a few words over it, and the end of it burst into magical flames, which cast light but no heat.

Moyra's face fell. "I—I think so."

"We have to try," Driskoll said, glancing back to make sure Latislav was coming with them.

Then a voice that Driskoll recognized said something in a language he couldn't understand. The sound alone made him shiver. He stared down the stairwell, past Moyra and Kellach, and saw a number of goblins standing at the bottom landing, torches in hand. The viceroy stood at the head of the pack, pointing at the Knights and shouting something in his guttural tongue.

16

The viceroy dashed forward, his arms stretched wide, and flung them around Kellach's waist. Driskoll dashed down the stairs, drawing his sword as he went. He readied it for a stabbing attack, right under his brother's arm. If the viceroy wouldn't let Kellach go, then Driskoll would make him.

The viceroy sprang back from the apprentice, wearing a wide grin on his face. The goblin leader bore a long cut along his cheek. Someone had stitched it up with material that looked sturdy enough to serve as a shoelace. Despite this, he looked happier than Driskoll had ever seen him. The goblins arrayed behind their king kept glancing back over their shoulders and eyeing Latislav and the young Knights with suspicious eyes. This didn't distract the Goblin King at all.

"The Goblin King welcomes us back to his realm," Kellach said.

"King?" Moyra said, pointing at the short, orange-skinned creature as he puffed out his chest with pride. "He's regained his throne?"

Kellach asked the Goblin King something in the creature's native tongue. The Goblin King listened carefully and then shrugged as he replied, still happy. He kept talking as Kellach translated.

"Not quite yet," Kellach said. "Their experiences in the chamber of the Great Seal convinced the goblins that life is too short to spend it under the collective thumb of a bunch of hobgoblins, so they launched a rebellion on the spot. So far it seems to be succeeding."

"What are these beasts doing out here then?" Latislav asked, looking walleyed at the goblins before him.

"Looking for you. They ran into Zendric and Mom. They told the goblins you might need some help—wait, that's 'could *be* some help'—so they came up to ask for your aid."

"Why aren't you with them, with Zendric and Jourdain?" Moyra asked, narrowing her eyes at the cleric.

"The demons harmed me. Zendric ordered me to stay behind and to protect their rear flank. Once I managed to erect the circle of protection, I healed myself through the graces of St. Cuthbert's eternal wisdom."

"Can they take us to the chamber?" Driskoll said.

"Of course," Kellach said, grinning. "That was the first thing I asked them. Let's go!"

Kellach said something to the Goblin King, and the little

leader leaped with excitement. He launched himself to the front of his pack of warriors and beckoned for the humans to follow close behind. They did, and the other goblins fell in right after them.

After following the Goblin King through a mind-bending array of twists and turns through the Dungeons of Doom, it occurred to Driskoll that they were trusting a goblin king and his army to guide them through a dungeon. Although he'd been relieved to have someone show them the way through the place, his inherent distrust of the creatures made him wonder if they were really so desperate as to place their lives in the hands of these small monsters.

From the grumblings coming from low in Latislav's throat, the cleric shared Driskoll's misgivings. More than once, though, Driskoll counted himself happy that the goblins didn't understand the common tongue. Otherwise, he guessed that the cleric's comments would have lost them their friendly guides.

They had to be getting close to the chamber. Driskoll didn't remember it being a terribly long march, just one he hoped never to have to make again. He kept telling himself that the chamber would be just around the next turn. Despite the fact that they took what seemed like dozens of such turns, the chamber never showed up. Then the Goblin King led them around a turn into a large, natural cavern that seemed to stretch on forever. The light of the goblins' torches could not reach the ceiling, or even the opposite wall.

"I remember this place," Moyra said. "It's not far now."

A horrible noise erupted from the far end of the cavern right then. Driskoll almost jumped out of his boots. The Goblin King listened to the sound and then responded with a screeching reply that was, if anything, worse to listen to than the initial sound. The other goblins moved up to band around him, their spears at the ready. Some of them handed their torches to the young Knights as they hefted their weapons and began to rattle them at their unseen foes.

"This can't be good," Moyra said.

"It's the Hobgoblin King," Kellach said.

As he spoke, a dozen faces crept up to the edge of the light cast by the goblins' torches. They looked much like those of the goblins, only larger and meaner, with far sharper fangs. They stood taller than Kellach, and they carried steel swords instead of wooden spears. The largest of the hobgoblins stood in the center of the group, right behind their front line. He growled low at the goblins as he adjusted the crown on his head.

"We don't have time for this," Driskoll said. "Mom and Zendric must be at the gate already!"

"Can you lead us to the chamber from here?" Kellach asked Moyra.

She nodded.

Kellach said something to the Goblin King, who turned and saluted. Taken aback, Kellach managed to snap back a salute of his own. Then he turned and grabbed Driskoll and Moyra's elbows.

"Let's go," he said. "The goblins will make sure the hobgoblins don't trouble us."

"What about them?" Moyra asked.

"If Mom and Zendric manage to use the Key of Order, they'll be a lot worse off," Driskoll said.

The three of them hustled off to the right, Latislav in their wake. As they left the chamber through an open portal in that right wall, the Goblin King led his loyal soldiers in a wall-rattling war cry, and the goblins charged into battle. Despite his dislike for the goblins, Driskoll found that he wished the Goblin King well. When compared to hobgoblins, at least, goblins didn't seem so bad.

"How much farther?" Kellach asked.

"Just three more turns, and we're there," Moyra said.

"Hold, children," Latislav said. "Please." He'd been dragging farther and farther behind since they'd left the goblins behind. Driskoll was ready to leave the old man behind if he couldn't keep up with them. Saving Curston was far more important than anyone else's ego.

"What is it?" Moyra said, as she turned back toward the panting cleric. She didn't bother to disguise the frustration in her voice.

"I can't permit you to go any farther," the cleric said, straightening up.

"Don't bother yourself with our welfare," Driskoll said. "We can handle ourselves."

Latislav nodded and then said, "That's just what I'm afraid

of. You three have proven yourself to be far more resourceful and capable than I would have guessed. You've been a thorn in my side for that very reason, and it's time for that to end."

Driskoll gaped. For a moment, he couldn't understand the meaning of Latislav's words. They sounded like a threat.

Moyra launched herself at the cleric. A knife that she had pulled from somewhere flashed out at him, like a claw tipping her hand. The cleric blocked Moyra's lunge with one arm and then reached out and touched her with the other. The reddish glow that had appeared around his hand leaped from his fingers to her cheek, and her eyes rolled back up into her head. She howled in pain and crumbled to her knees.

Kellach began to chant something, but Latislav snarled at him.

"Silence!" the cleric said. His hand glowed red once more, and he held it over the crumpled Moyra. "One more syllable, and I'll kill her."

Driskoll gasped. "Lexos didn't tamper with the Key of Order at all. It was you!"

Latislav grinned, his eyes dancing with evil. "And how fortunate it was for me that you children stumbled into the church just as I had finished my work. I had wondered if I could convince Jourdain and Zendric to accept the Key so readily, but you completed that task for me."

"You've been working with Lexos all along," Kellach said. He stuck out his jaw and shook his head, his face flushed with shame. "I've been such a fool."

"You and everyone else in Curston," Latislav said. "Do you know how hard it's been for me to play the obsequious servant of St. Cuthbert for all these long months? All the while, knowing that someday, with my help, my dark master would rise to devour the town?"

"Won't you just be killed too?" Driskoll said.

He had to keep the man talking to buy time. Moyra moaned softly as she rolled on the floor, holding her head in her hands. On the other hand, Driskoll knew their time was running out. If they didn't do something quick, his mother and Zendric would use the Key of Order, and it would be too late.

"You sold out the entire city," Kellach said. "For what?"

"Power, boy," Latislav said, leering at the apprentice. He seemed content to let the last bits of sand flow through the hourglass. "Power and immortality and the chance to make the most of them both. What more could a man want?"

Moyra reached up at that moment and drove her knife into Latislav's belly. The cleric doubled over and howled in pain and surprise. The glow on his hand faded as he clutched at his wound and pulled at the knife still stuck there. Moyra let go of the knife and fell back to the ground. Her attack seemed to have taken the last bit of her energy. Driskoll wanted to rush to her side, to see if she was all right, but he sensed that they were out of time.

"Mom!" Driskoll cupped his hands around his lips and shouted, as he stepped away from the others and toward the chamber. He thought he knew the way from here. Even if he couldn't find them, maybe they could hear him at least.

"Zendric!" Driskoll shouted, his voice echoing down the tunnel. "Don't use the Key! Stop!"

A horrible crack sounded from somewhere up ahead. It rang through the passageway so loudly that Driskoll wondered if Guffy might have been able to hear it all the way at the entrance to the Dungeons of Doom.

Kellach grabbed Driskoll by his collar and hauled him back to where Moyra lay crumpled on the floor.

"We have to stick together!" Kellach shouted. He said some other things, but Driskoll couldn't make them out.

Driskoll held his ears to block out the noise. Then something louder, and far worse, sounded down the passage: the blast of a horrible horn that could only have come from the depths of the Abyss.

CHAPTER

17

Latislav staggered down the hallway past Driskoll. He held on to his belly with both hands, the knife still embedded there, as he stumbled past Driskoll and into the twisting passageways beyond. The chamber that held the Great Seal was only three turns away, or so Moyra had said. Latislav would be there in moments and claim his long-awaited reward.

Driskoll glanced back and saw Kellach kneeling over Moyra, who still lay in a heap on the floor. Even in the flickering torchlight, Driskoll could see how pale she looked. It was too late to save his mother, or Zendric, or Curston, Driskoll knew, but maybe not too late for Moyra. He pulled himself to his feet and scrambled over to her, putting his hand on his brother's shoulder.

"Is she dead?" Driskoll asked.

Kellach held her head in one hand and was sweeping the hair from her face with the other. She looked angry, not filled with the peace of the dead but the rage of the wronged. Driskoll wondered if her spirit would haunt him and Kellach forever.

Then Moyra coughed and opened her bright green eyes. The fire in them had not faded, although dark circles rimmed them.

"Can you stand?" Kellach asked.

She nodded, and Driskoll offered her his hand. He pulled her to her feet while Kellach pushed. She fell into Driskoll's arms, still unsteady for a moment, and then straightened herself out, blowing the hair out of her face.

"I feel like I got run over by a wagon," Moyra said, as she tried to stretch the kinks out of her back and limbs. "But I think I'll live."

"We need to get out of here," Driskoll said.

"And go where?" asked Kellach. "Back to Curston?"

"We could flee into the woods. If we can make it to the main road, we might be able to get to the towns west of here before Curston falls. Maybe they can send help."

"Or at least make their own defenses ready," said Moyra.

Kellach shook his head. "Curston is the most-fortified, best-protected city in the entire region. If it falls, then the others have no chance. The demon horde will march straight over them."

"Then we'll just keep running ahead of them," Driskoll said. "Eventually someone will be able to make a stand against them, right? They can't just run straight to the sea."

Kellach grimaced. "Don't you think we ought to look for Mom and Zendric first?"

Driskoll flushed with shame. "Do you think there's any . . . hope?" he asked. He barely dared to even speak the word.

"There's always hope," Moyra said. "Right up until the end."

She limped forward, not glancing back at the boys. They looked at each other and then fell into step behind her. They made it past one turn, then the second. As they neared the third, they watched as one humongous demon after another marched, wriggled, or slithered past. The creatures worked their way through the larger tunnel, where the passage the kids were in led. The demons rarely bothered to look to their left to see the kids standing in the narrow passage.

One of the creatures stopped for a moment at the mouth of the passage and leered at the young Knights. Saliva dripped from its fangs as it licked its wide crimson lips. Its long tongue lashed out only to fall several feet shy of the Knights. Still, Driskoll jumped at the first flick, and only Kellach's hand on his arm kept him from racing off in the other direction.

Soon, the creature was forced to move forward as something shoved it from behind. As it did, Driskoll heard a scream. For an instant, he feared it might be his mother or Zendric. Then he recognized the hated voice. It belonged to Latislav.

"No!" the cleric screeched. "We had a bargain! No!"

As the Knights watched, Latislav appeared in the mouth of the passageway, borne in the clutches of a gigantic demon. The massive beast had the skin of an armored toad, covered with dozens of wicked spines that ran along the length of its arms, legs, and skulls. It carried the cleric like a hated child, its fist large enough to fit entirely around the cleric's chest.

"Children!" Latislav shrieked, as the demon dragged him past. "Save me! *Save me!*"

Then the demon flexed its fist, squeezing the cleric tight, and Latislav said no more.

"How many of them can there be?" Moyra asked, shuddering.

Driskoll looked at Kellach, whose eyes stretched wide. "Still don't think we should leave?" he asked.

Kellach shivered and then seemed to come back to himself. "Mom spent five years in the Abyss. If anyone can survive against these monsters, she can." He glared at his little brother. "And we waited five years for her to come back to us. I think we can be patient a bit longer if we must."

Driskoll nodded reluctantly. The thought that they might run into the demons on their way out of the Dungeons of Doom had occurred to him too. At least here in the tunnel, they were safe—for the moment. It didn't seem like anywhere was really safe anymore.

"They're gone," Moyra said. She had crept down the tunnel until she reached its lip.

"How can you say that?" said Driskoll. "I can still hear them." The sounds of a battle reached his ears from somewhere off in the darkness.

"Wait," said Kellach, "if someone's still fighting, that means Mom and Zendric—"

"Are still alive!" Driskoll said. "Let's go!"

Moyra was already racing down the wide passageway, the final stretch that led to the chamber of the Great Seal. Kellach sprinted after her with Driskoll pumping his legs in their wake.

When Driskoll reached the chamber, he had to push between Moyra and Kellach to force his way in. They had stopped in the entranceway, stunned. Once Driskoll got past them, he saw why.

Zendric and Jourdain stood arrayed against a massive demon that looked like it had sprung straight out of Driskoll's worst nightmares. It towered over the two wizards at twice their height. Long wings stretched out even farther from its shoulders, scraping against the ceiling as they filled the chamber from side to side. A mane of dark red hair fell back from a face that resembled a skinned bull. Long, sharp horns the color of scorched bones jutted from each side of its head where its ears should have been. Its crimson skin shimmered in the flickering light of its jagged, flaming sword. In its other hand, it cracked a whip that seemed to be made wholly of fire, but that flexed and flicked like supple leather.

Zendric zapped the creature again and again with his wand. Icy rays of pure, freezing cold lanced the demon's skin, turning it black where the blows fell. Meanwhile, Jourdain angled around at the creature, a small, glassy globe in her hands. Driskoll recognized it by the gold bands around it: the spiritkeeper.

The demon roared something at the wizards in its unfathomable tongue, and Driskoll felt his legs freeze to the ground.

"It's a balor," Kellach said, his voice barely more than a whisper. "We're doomed."

"I don't think we needed to know its name to figure that out," Moyra said.

The balor's whip scarred the walls and ceiling of the chamber as it lashed out with wild abandon. Then it came back and wrapped around Jourdain's waist.

"Mom!" Driskoll shouted. He found himself running forward, reaching for her as the demon pulled her up into the air by the whip.

Driskoll watched in horror as the spiritkeeper slipped from his mother's hands. Moyra whizzed past Driskoll again. She dived forward and plucked the transparent globe from the air before it could smash into a hundred shiny, useless pieces.

The balor used its whip to haul Jourdain up toward its face.

Jourdain screamed.

Driskoll had never felt so helpless in his life. He clenched his fists. Here he'd waited for five long years for his mother to come back to him, and now he had to watch her die at the hands of one of the demons she'd battled for so long. And he couldn't do a thing about it.

Moyra glanced his way and seemed to read his mind. "There's only one thing you can do."

"What?"

Moyra tossed the spiritkeeper to Driskoll. "Catch!"

18

F or the first time in a long time, Driskoll knew exactly
what to do.

He'd been forced to use the spiritkeeper once before to put
Zendric's soul into Kellach's body. Back then he hadn't been
sure he could make the magic work. Now, faced with the same
task, Driskoll didn't hesitate for an instant. He thrust the spiritkeeper forward at the demon and shouted out the magic word
engraved on the globe's golden base.

"Animamedere!"

A vortex of glowing smoke shot from the spiritkeeper and
enveloped the balor. The demon roared as its essence was torn
from its body. It fought against it, screaming and writhing the
whole way. It dropped its sword and whip, and Jourdain landed
hard on the unforgiving ground. Driskoll wanted to go to his
mother, to make sure she was okay, but if he did that now it
would doom them all.

Sweat beaded on Driskoll's forehead and began to drip down his face. The heat from the creature and its weapons was horrible, but the effort to haul the balor's soul in was even worse. Driskoll didn't know if he could manage it. He felt his will ebbing away from him, draining from him with his last bit of strength.

Then he felt Moyra's hands on his.

"How does this thing work?" she shouted at him over the balor's furious howls.

"Don't ask me!" Driskoll said, shaking his head. He was glad to have Moyra there, trying to lend him her strength, but it didn't seem to have any direct effect.

"It's not enough!" Driskoll said after a moment. "I can't make it work!"

Then Kellach placed his hands over Moyra and Driskoll's.

"Animamedere!" the apprentice said, adding his will to that of his brother and their friend.

Driskoll felt the determination of the others rush through him and into the globe between his hands. He glanced up at Kellach, but his brother was too focused on the crimson smoke swirling around the balor to look back.

"Animamedere!" Driskoll said once more.

He turned his head and saw Moyra flashing him a determined grin. For a moment, he thought she might even start laughing. Together, the two younger knights looked at Kellach. Sweat streamed down his face now too, just as it did with the others. He seemed to sense them staring at him and turned, half-surprised. He nodded at them, and they all knew what to do.

"*Animamedere!*" they all shouted as one.

The demon threw back its head and unleashed a horrifying scream as its essence streamed from its massive body and collected into the spiritkeeper. The balor's body hung there in front of the gate for a moment then came tumbling down with a horrible thud that snapped one of its horns off at its base.

Driskoll stared at the gold-banded ball in his hands and watched the smoke swirling angrily within, as if he'd managed to capture a hurricane within its fragile grasp. Carrying it with great care, he trotted over to where Kellach was helping their mother to her feet.

"Are you all right?" Kellach asked.

Jourdain grimaced as she struggled to her feet. She could move, but only with great pain. Her left arm hung limp at her side. "I'll live," she said, "if only barely."

Kellach put her right arm over his shoulder and let her lean on him. Driskoll noticed then that Kellach was as tall as Jourdain. Driskoll's memories of his mother were all at least five years old, and she'd had more than a head on Kellach even in the most recent of those days. Now, though, her eldest son stood as an equal to her, in height if not maturity or power.

"I can't believe our foolishness," Zendric said, as he came over to Jourdain and the boys. He'd shrugged off Moyra's insistence on inspecting his injuries, despite the tears and cuts on his face and arms.

"We were meant to be fooled," Jourdain said. "Lexos fooled us all—again."

"He had Latislav's help this time," Kellach said. "We couldn't have known."

"You couldn't have," Zendric said, glancing back at the gate. "But I should have."

The portal into the Abyss stood twice as tall and wide as before now, large enough that the balor had passed through it with ease. The creature's body partly blocked the opening now, but Driskoll knew that this wouldn't be enough to stop another of its kind from charging through the opening at will.

"We have to get back the city," Jourdain said, wincing at every word. "We have to evacuate."

Zendric shook his head. "It's already too late. The demons will reach it before we do. Our only hope is to awaken the dragons."

"What good will that do?" asked Jourdain. "With the gate wide open, the demons will continue to stream through, and the dragons will all die too. Better to leave them to sleep through this horror. Maybe they can rebuild after this is all over."

"What if we could repair the Key?" Kellach said. He reached inside the folds of his robes as he spoke.

Zendric scowled. "Impossible, I'd think. To do that, we'd need—Ah!"

Kellach withdrew Lochinvar from where he'd been hiding in a pocket inside the robes, and he presented the dragonet to Zendric.

"I see," said Zendric, as he touched Lochinvar's wings. "This is how you realized the Key we had was tainted."

Kellach nodded. "Can you use his wings to fix it?"

Zendric frowned as he worked the slender, silvery wings off of Lochinvar's back. "Possibly," he said. The wizard knelt down on the rocky floor and began to work.

As he did, Jourdain reached out and stroked her sons' faces with her good hand. "I've never been so proud," she said. "You boys did the right thing."

Then Jourdain squinted at Kellach and Driskoll. "Does your father know you're here?"

The boys both looked away.

"I didn't think so," Jourdain said.

"But, Mom," Driskoll said. "There wasn't any time. Guffy can back us up on that."

"Guffy's here?" she asked, surprised.

Kellach nodded. "He got hurt while helping us fight our way in here past some demons near the entrance. We left him in the circle of protection there."

Jourdain took in a pained breath. "Driskoll," she said, "can you reach into my pocket and pull out the first vial on the left?"

Without a word, Driskoll plunged his hand into her pocket. Just as he remembered from his childhood, it was ten times as large inside as out. He'd hidden in there once as a young boy, long before the Sundering of the Seal, and it had taken his parents an hour of searching to find him. He found the steel vial that Jourdain had asked for, and plucked it from the pocket. Blue wax covered its cork, sealing it solid.

"Open that for me, please," she said.

Moyra handed Driskoll a knife, which he used to cut the wax seal and pry out the cork. "I thought you lost your knife in Latislav's belly," he said.

"I always carry a spare," Moyra said, not a hint of smugness in her voice.

Driskoll handed the open vial to Jourdain who accepted it with a tiny smile and drank it. Within moments, her arm could move again, and the scent of scorched flesh that had followed her faded.

"That's better," Jourdain said, as she recorked the vial and replaced it in her pocket. "I'll save the rest for Guffy."

Lochinvar, wingless once more, skittered over to Kellach and nuzzled against the boy's legs until his master picked him up. He slithered into place atop Kellach's shoulder and purred a ticking sound.

As Jourdain looked up at the young Knights, her brow creased with concern. "Where's Zendric?" she asked.

Driskoll glanced about and saw that the portal into the Abyss had started to glow with a pure, white light. He pointed toward it, but Jourdain was already dashing toward it.

"No!" she shouted. "Zendric, you can't do this!"

The young Knights followed Jourdain over to the portal, stepping over the body of the balor as they did. For a moment, Driskoll worried that the creature might sit up and devour him, but he refused to let his fear keep him from helping his mother. As Driskoll peered down the widened tunnel that led to the larger gate, he saw a shimmering sheet of light covering its surface like a drape between the two worlds. Through it, he saw Zendric standing on the other side, holding the Key of Order before him.

"Hurry!" the wizard shouted. "I can't hold this up by myself forever!"

19

Z endric!" Jourdain shouted. "Come back here now! We'll figure out some other way to remake the Seal this time."

"No time for that, I'm afraid," Zendric called from the other side of the veil of light. "I scouted out of the cavern here, and there's another army of demons already coming this way. They'll be here soon, and there's only one possible way to stop them."

"Trade places with me," Jourdain said. "I know the Abyss. I lived and fought there. I have the best chance to survive."

Zendric shook his head, a wry smile on his lips. "I let you use that line of logic on me the last time around, my dear. I allowed circumstances to separate you from your husband and your sons.

"They're good boys—I daresay great even—but they've had to grow up without you. And you without them. I won't let that happen again."

"Zendric!" Jourdain spluttered for a moment, struggling for something to say. Then she fell silent for a moment. When she spoke again, her voice sounded firm and steady.

"Thank you," she said.

"Cast your half of the spell," Zendric said. "Or I will have trapped myself over here for no reason."

The old elf smiled at Jourdain. "Quickly, please," he said. "You know how to work this. After all, we've done it before."

Jourdain put on a grim face and set to work. Kellach watched her every move, studying her as she went about crafting and completing her end of the spell, which Zendric had already started.

"So," Moyra said, keeping her voice low so as to not disturb Jourdain, "are we all Knights of the Silver Dragon again?"

"I never stopped," said Driskoll. They both looked at Kellach.

The apprentice pretended not to notice them for a moment. When it became clear they wouldn't leave off watching him, he turned and scowled at them. "What?"

Driskoll reached into his pocket and pulled out something small and sharp. He extended his hand toward his brother, letting the item lay there, sparkling. Kellach looked down to see his silver dragon pin sitting in the palm of Driskoll's hand. He smiled at it, touched.

"You picked it up."

Driskoll tried to hold back a grin, but failed. "You didn't think I'd let you out of the order that easy, did you?"

Kellach took the pin from Driskoll's hand and attached it to his robes, tattered as they were, with even a sleeve missing. Moyra and Driskoll smiled at him, and the three put their arms around one another in a quick embrace.

"My Knights!" Zendric called.

Moyra, Kellach, and Driskoll, each wearing a pin now, turned to peer through the thickening veil at the wizard on the others side. "Yes, Zendric?" Kellach said, his voice raw.

"I leave Curston in your capable hands. The Knights who have returned—including your mother—will need your help. They have been gone long enough to forget many things. There is much you can teach each other."

Don't do this, Driskoll wanted to say. *We need you here.* But he knew that if there had been another path Zendric would have taken it—or Jourdain would have forced him along it. To complain about something that could not be changed seemed like whining, and Driskoll was determined to make sure that Zendric didn't hear such things from him.

Jourdain kept chanting and gesturing in the mysterious way of wizards. Driskoll knew he would never understand such things fully, nor did he care to learn. Right now, all he needed to know he saw on his mother's face: the grim determination as she sealed her friend and mentor in the hellish prison of the Abyss.

Jourdain finished her side of the spell with a flourish. As she did, she drew something from her robes and tossed it through the nearly solid veil. Shiny and flat, with a golden rim, it seemed to stick in the coagulating Seal for a moment, then something—or someone—plucked it through from the other side.

"Good-bye, Jourdain!" Zendric's voice called through the grayish substance, the sound almost completely muffled. "Farewell, my Knights! Kellach, Driskoll, and Moyra. May the Silver Dragons keep you well!"

Jourdain started forward and thrust her hand into the mist. "No!" she shouted. "There's still a chance for you! Come back!" Her arm disappeared into the thick swirls of gray. She pulled it back a moment later, with Zendric's wrist clamped in her fist.

The young Knights rushed to the Seal, but when Driskoll tried to reach through it, he only ended up with bruised fingertips for his trouble. The Seal was now as solid as could be. The only exception to that seemed to be the bits that touched directly on Zendric's arm. Then the arm wrenched out of Jourdain's grasp and was gone. It fell back through the Seal with an audible *pop*.

Jourdain fell back onto the ground and buried her face in her hands. Her shoulders shook with her silent sobs, and Kellach and Driskoll both hugged her.

"We don't have time for this," Moyra said. "We may have finally remade the Seal—although it's anyone's guess for how long—but all those monstrous demons who walked past us are on their way to Curston. We need to figure out how to stop them."

Driskoll scowled. "Can't you give our mother a chance?" he asked. "She's been through a lot."

"Who hasn't?" Moyra said, not a hint of apology in her tone. "I'm glad we've rescued your mother, but *my* mother's still out there in Curston, as are our fathers—and the whole city. If we have a prayer of saving them, we need to move now."

"And just what do you suggest we do?" Driskoll said. "If we go back to Curston now, it'll only be to die alongside all those other people. There's nothing we can do, not a single thing."

"No," Jourdain said, as she pulled herself to her feet. "There's still a way. The Knights of the Silver Dragon were created for this moment, to be able to put into action a plan to save the city from the worst horrors you could imagine."

"That's what it says in the Prophecy of the Dragons," said Kellach. He looked up at the ceiling while he searched his memory. "There's a passage that says, 'And in the city's darkest hour, the knights will call upon a higher power.' Do you know what that means?"

Jourdain cocked her head at her eldest son. "Zendric never told you?" she asked.

Kellach shook his head, as did Driskoll and Moyra.

"Well," Jourdain said, as she headed for the chamber's exit. "Now we have something interesting to talk about on our march back to the city."

20

The young knights and Jourdain only made it halfway back to the exit from the Dungeons of Doom when they ran into the goblins again. Driskoll had started to think that perhaps Jourdain and Moyra didn't know their way around the place as well as they claimed, that maybe they were lost and might never find their way out of the labyrinthine place. That's about when he noticed they were surrounded.

"They're getting smarter," Kellach said, as he peered out at the diminutive creatures coming at them from both directions in the small chamber into which the passageway had opened.

The Goblin King bounded toward the young Knights and wrapped his arms around Kellach's legs. Driskoll noticed that the Goblin King had regained his crown. It was battered and bent but still recognizable as a crown, and it sat on the creature's head at a skewed but proud angle.

The Goblin King turned to his subjects and presented Jourdain and the young Knights to them with a flourish and a bow. As he did, the other goblins raised their spears and rattled them in what Driskoll could only guess was their version of a raucous cheer.

"They seem far fonder of us than they used to be," Driskoll said, as the Goblin King turned back and started speaking to Kellach in fast, staccato sentences.

"It seems the Goblin King has told his subject that we're responsible for all those demons getting loose," said Kellach. Jourdain nodded at her son, impressed.

"I suppose he's right about that," said Moyra, "but why would that make them happy?"

Kellach grinned as he spoke with the Goblin King. "You remember how they entered their final battle against the hobgoblins? Well, when those massive demons came through here, they wiped out the hobgoblins. The goblins managed to hide away in niches and passages that were too small for the demons to follow them into."

"Just like us," Moyra said.

"So we're heroes to them?" Jourdain said, with a wry smile. "Can you get them to guide us to the exit?"

Kellach said something to the Goblin King, and the leader grinned at him with his wide rows of teeth. Then he turned and shouted something to his subjects, who raised and rattled their spears once more. Then they parted before the young Knights and Jourdain. The Goblin King ran before them, leading the way to the exit. What seemed like every survivor of the goblin kingdom tromped along with them. They soon reached the surface where they found Guffy sitting in the middle of the circle of protection. The quasits still hovered overhead, hurling curses at any humans or goblins in range.

Jourdain gestured at each of the quasits in turn, and the horrible beasts jerked upward as if something had bitten them on the rump. Then they turned and flew off, dodging left and right like drunken bumble-bats, squealing the whole way.

Kellach took the half-used potion from Jourdain's pocket and uncorked it for Guffy. As the sergeant swallowed it, his scorched hair began to grow back, and his skin lost its slick, burnt sheen.

"I'm sorry," Kellach said to Guffy. "That's all there is."

"Then it'll have to be enough," Guffy said, with a strained grin.

"What happened to the demons?" Moyra asked.

"What do you mean?" Guffy asked. "They ran right through here as if their wings were on fire. I nearly wet myself. I'd have run off gibbering into the night if I'd been able to get my legs to work that well."

"The circle of protection is still intact," Jourdain said. "How did they get past you?"

Guffy pointed to a large hole some distance off, near the edge of the square closest to the road back to Curston. Now that Driskoll looked at it, he wondered how any of them could have missed it. It had to be forty feet across, and smoke continued to curl up out of it, as if it still burned.

"They tried to come up the stairs, but they couldn't fit," said Guffy. "So they made their own exit over there."

"How in the world are we going to stop that?" Driskoll said in an awed voice.

■ ▮ █ ▮ █

"We need to get to Main Square," Jourdain said as they approached the city of Curston. They'd made good time getting back to the city from the Dungeons of Doom—almost too good.

Guffy had transformed into a werewolf again and carried the children the whole way. Jourdain had raced alongside them, keeping pace well.

Even from a quarter mile off, Driskoll could see the humongous demons smashing into the Westgate over and over again. He had no doubt that they would soon bring it crashing down. When they did, the land-bound creatures would join their winged brethren inside the city's walls. Curston would not last long after that.

Instead of trying to confront the massive creatures directly, Jourdain had led them around the city toward the now-peaceful Oldgate. When they reached it, Guffy brought Jourdain and Moyra up and over the wall first. Kellach and Driskoll waited for him to return on the ground outside the wall, standing in the halo of light cast by the torches burning high around the gate.

"I knew you couldn't quit the Knights forever," Driskoll said.

"Shut up." Kellach put an arm around his little brother. "What is it you always say to me? 'Just because you're right doesn't mean you have to rub it in.'"

The werewolf landed with a thud right before them. Without a word, or even a growl, the creature snatched them up and clambered over the wall. As they topped the battlements, a squad of watchers stared up at them in horror. Despite this, they kept their weapons to themselves and let the creature and his cargo pass. Guffy placed the boys down next to Moyra and their mother and grunted at them all.

Jourdain put a hand on the werewolf's arm. "The watchers said that they managed to repel the demons—all but the flying ones, of course. Torin came by with a force of his finest fighters, searching for stragglers trying to come over the walls in some of the more remote parts of the city. He seemed of good cheer.

"Then the large demons arrived. Torin ordered some of the watchers to come with him and left a small crew here to guard the Oldgate. They ran toward the Westgate no more than a quarter hour ago. The battle has raged there ever since."

The thought of his father leading the effort to save the city from those monstrous demons twisted Driskoll's stomach in a knot. He didn't see how any mortal army—even the vaunted watchers of Curston—could hope to prevail against those creatures, no matter how many blades they brought to bear.

"We have to go help him!" Driskoll said.

Jourdain gave her youngest son a grim look, but before she could open her mouth, a horrible crash sounded from the northwest. Driskoll thought he could feel it shake the ground even from there.

"The Westgate is breached!" a watcher shouted from atop the wall. "The Westgate is breached. The demons are charging in!"

CHAPTER

21

W e have no time to lose," Jourdain said, as she sprinted off
to the north. "We need to reach Main Square now."

"Main Square?" Driskoll said, as he chased after her with
Moyra and Kellach right behind. "Why? The fighting's at the
Westgate—and so is Dad!"

Guffy leaped away from the young Knights, taking to the
roof. As he loped along above and alongside them, the werewolf
scanned the region for stray demons, making sure that none lay
in ambush.

"The battle may be there, but the solution is not," Jourdain said. "The watchers cannot hope to stand against the
demons. I fought them for five years, and standing toe-to-toe
with them is nothing short of suicide for any but the greatest
of heroes."

She turned back to look at her sons. "I count your father in
those ranks. However, he is a good and loyal leader who will

not leave his watchers to fend for themselves. If we don't find some help for him soon, they will all be killed."

Jourdain led the young Knights north through the Phoenix Quarter. This part of town had been destroyed after the first Sundering of the Seal. It now featured the newest and nicest buildings in town, all reinforced against such attacks, but Driskoll doubted any of them could withstand the full force of this latest demonic assault. This quarter only served to remind him how much damage the creatures could do, how they'd almost razed Curston to the ground the last time.

Driskoll had only been seven years old at the time, and he'd been terrified out of his mind. Jourdain had gone missing after running off to help Zendric remake the Seal. Torin had been mortally wounded as well. Only Lexos's intervention had saved the man, leaving the boys with at least one parent to raise them amid the smoking ruins of a city left in the aftermath of battle. Driskoll had cried himself to sleep every night for months after that. Torin had comforted him the best he could, but the captain of the watch had always been more of a fighter than a father. In any case, no one could have replaced Jourdain in her sons' hearts, and Torin had been wise enough to not even try.

Over time, the boys had learned to soldier on without their mother. They lived almost as guests in their own home, the place that Torin had rebuilt from the ashes of the old. He'd insisted on it looking just like it had before the destruction. He never said anything to his sons, but Driskoll had always suspected that his father wanted it to stand ready for their mother, a familiar hearth and home for her if and when she should ever return.

As they raced through the Phoenix Quarter, they passed by that house. Everburning torches flickered in the sconces set outside the windows, lighting the place all around, at any time of day. Jourdain had barely been back to the place, but already it seemed more like a real home to Driskoll. He wondered if the place would ever see all four members of his family gathered together in it again.

"Why Main Square?" said Moyra. "What's so important there?"

"The Great Circle," Jourdain said.

"It's a gigantic circle of protection," Driskoll said. "We know. We used it the night we first fought Lexos."

Jourdain arched an eyebrow at her youngest son. "When this is all over, we need to sit down and chat. I think we have a lot of catching up to do."

"But we can't just sit out the battle in the Great Circle," said Kellach. "We can't just wait for the demons to bring Curston down around our ears."

"That's not the plan," Jourdain said. "There's more to the Great Circle than its protective nature. Have you ever wondered what the obelisk is for?"

Driskoll hadn't. To him, it was just the easiest landmark to spot in the town. It stood taller than any other building, including Zendric's tower and the Cathedral of St. Cuthbert.

If Driskoll could spot a part of the city wall and the obelisk, it meant he could find his way home.

"It's not just part of a giant sundial?" Moyra said.

"That's part of it," Jourdain said. "It keeps track of time in the city, marking the hours for those who built it. But it's more than that. Much more."

"What?" the three young Knights said in unison.

"It's a marker—a grave marker."

Driskoll stumbled and nearly fell, but Moyra caught his arm. They ran on.

"Who's buried there?" Kellach asked.

At that moment, a trio of incubi swung down from the sky. Driskoll saw them swooping at them, the light from the burning rooftops picking them out like fireflies in the night sky.

"Look out!" Moyra said, pointing at the creatures.

Driskoll's eyes darted about, looking for a place to hide. But nothing showed itself. Anyway, his mother hadn't stopped running toward Main Square, which he could now see was opening up before them. If they could make it through the market and into the Great Circle, they'd be safe. But the demons were gaining on them too fast. Driskoll knew that his legs would never bring him to safety in time.

"Mom!" he shouted, as panic climbed from his heart to his head.

Jourdain slowed her pace and reached back for Driskoll and Kellach, taking their hands in hers. Moyra zipped past all three of them. As she did, she glanced back behind them and cheered.

A terrifying snarl rent the air overhead. Driskoll looked up to see Guffy launch himself from a nearby rooftop and smash into the path of incubi. The werewolf grabbed two of the creatures in his mighty paws and smashed bodily into a third.

"Keep running!" Jourdain said.

They followed Moyra as she dived into the abandoned booths of the bazaar. She twisted and turned her way through them with a speed borne of hundreds of hours lacing her way through the place in the middle of the busiest days. Driskoll feared he might lose sight of her, but she peered back over her shoulder to make sure that he, his mother, and his brother were managing to keep up.

When they reached the inner edge of the market, they charged straight on into it. Driskoll noticed that the tiny, burning obelisks that Zendric had set up earlier were still there, their flames flickering in the breeze but never going out.

"Kellach," Jourdain said, "come with me. Driskoll and Moyra, sit tight. Whatever you do, don't leave the Great Circle."

Driskoll nodded, panting for breath as he and Moyra strolled up to the obelisk in the center of the circle. "Useless again," he said, once he managed to catch his breath.

"That's the way of the spell-less in these situations," Moyra said.

Driskoll stared at her. "Have you ever been in a situation like this before?" he asked.

She started to respond, but then giggled. He laughed along-side her for a moment. The sound seemed to beat back his fear of the creatures he knew hungered for them out there in the night.

"Now that's a noise I haven't heard in far too long," a tiny voice said from the other side of the obelisk.

Driskoll recognized it at once. "Gryphyll!" he said, as he dashed around the corner of the obelisk, Moyra on his heels.

There, waiting for them, stood a small creature that looked a bit like a caricature of a gnome. He was about the same height as the members of that tiny race—barely taller than a toddler—with tall, round ears that stood out from his head like wings, and his long bulbous nose stuck out like a beak. He wore the same clothes as he had the first time Driskoll had seen him, months before: a dirty, gray tunic over short pants, and curly toed shoes, plus a wide belt with a simple, silver buckle. And he had that same mysterious grin too, the one that said that he either knew far more than you could ever hope to—or that he was a complete idiot.

Driskoll marveled at Gryphyll and his complete disguise. If he hadn't seen the tiny man take his true form as a silver dragon before, he never would have believed it. The thought that a crea-ture as marvelous and beautiful as a silver dragon would ever voluntarily choose to look anything like what Gryphyll did now stunned Driskoll. He had to admit, though, that despite being a Knight of the Silver Dragon he knew precious little about such magnificent beings.

"What are you doing here?" Moyra said. She fingered a silver chain that hung around her neck, a gift the strange creature had given her when they'd last seen each other—after defeating Lexos and trapping him in Gryphyll's abandoned lair.

"A treasure! A treasure!" Gryphyll said, as he reached up to play with Moyra's hair with a long, thin finger. "I came here to help, of course. The great wizard Zendric called to me, and so I came." The creature stopped smiling for a moment. "I have not been able to find him though or reach him since."

"Oh, Gryphyll," Moyra said, "Zendric is—"

"Dead!" Lexos bellowed, as he charged into the Great Circle, straight toward Driskoll, Moyra, and Gryphyll. His head and shoulders crackled with barely contained energy that shifted in color from red to black and back. "And so shall you be too!"

CHAPTER

22

O h, Lexos!" Gryphyll said, clapping his hands together with glee. "You are such a treasure! So dramatic! So powerful! So sure of yourself!"

The grin on the creature's face infuriated the cleric. "Mock me if you will, dragon," he said with a snarl. "I know you now for who you are, and I am ready."

With that, Lexos spat out a single word. Although he barely seemed to move his lips or to raise his voice, it echoed painfully in Driskoll's ears. Still, there was some part of him that refused to listen to it, that shut it out, grateful that it didn't seem to be meant for him. Gryphyll, on the other hand, fell to his knees, clutching his ears and wailing in pain or misery—perhaps both.

Driskoll spotted Lexos coming straight for them, his lips moving as he chanted the words to another prayer to his dark god. Driskoll knew that the spell would mean the murder of the transformed dragon for sure.

"No!" Driskoll said, charging forward.

As he did, he drew the silver dagger that Gryphyll had given him. Its amethyst-studded handle felt right in his hand as he lunged at the cleric, as if it had been fashioned from the dragon's fang and would finally now be used for its destined purpose: to protect the life of one of its kind. The dagger's blade sliced out at Lexos, but the cleric proved faster than Driskoll remembered him. He dodged out of the dagger's path, and then backhanded Driskoll to the ground.

The blow sent stars flying before Driskoll's eyes. He shook his head, trying to clear his vision. When he finally managed it, he saw Moyra standing between Lexos and Gryphyll. She had her dagger out and at the ready, daring the man to take another step forward.

Lexos surged toward Moyra and slapped her weapon out of her hand. Then he hauled her up above his head with one arm and prepared to hurl her into the stands of the bazaar, just beyond the edge of the Great Circle—or maybe to dash her on the ground before him instead.

Driskoll had always thought of the cleric as fat and lazy. Only by magical means could he have become so strong and lethal in battle. The boy knew he'd never be able to reach the cleric in time to save Moyra, and even if he did, chances were good that Lexos would just kill him too.

"Gryphyll!" Driskoll called. "Help her!"

But the little man just rocked there on his knees, unable to do anything more than hold his head. Moyra would get no help from that quarter.

"Let her go!" Kellach said, as he raced from around the other side of the obelisk.

Lexos glanced back at the apprentice and laughed. He stopped dead, though, when he saw Jourdain appear from around the obelisk as well. Jourdain opened her mouth, and a horrible screech spat out of it. It warped the air as it lanced toward Lexos and caught him in the head. He dropped Moyra and nearly fell to his knees. She landed like a cat and rolled away as soon as she hit the ground. Lexos wiped away a streak of red that had tumbled from his ears.

"I've been waiting five years to finish you off," he said, already working another spell as he spoke. He rose into the air, then, beckoning for the wizard to follow him.

Jourdain tossed out a spell of her own and rose into the air after Lexos. As she went, she called down to Kellach, "You must complete our work."

"What's that supposed to mean?" Driskoll said, as he and Kellach rushed over to help Moyra and Gryphyll to their feet.

Kellach pointed to the blazing obelisks around the Great Circle's rim. "Zendric set up a spell here, something to save the town. Mom was about to cast it when Lexos showed up."

"I thought you were giving up magic," Moyra said. She looked down at Gryphyll, who had stopped rocking back and forth and holding his head in his hands. He uncurled from his knees and stood next to her, holding her hand.

"I rejoined the Knights of the Silver Dragon, didn't I?" said

Kellach. "I'll tell you what. If I blow this, I'll never mess with magic again."

"Really?" said Driskoll.

Kellach nodded. "I can't cast a thing if I'm dead."

The apprentice turned toward the obelisk and started to chant. He stumbled over the words at first, the nerves he normally kept under such tight control betraying him. As he spoke, though, he seemed to feel something flow through him, though whether it came from some magic source or deep within himself, Kellach couldn't say.

Meanwhile, off in the distance, a ball of fire exploded over the Cathedral of St. Cuthbert. Driskoll hoped to see Lexos falling to the ground, leaving a trail of flames behind him. Instead, the cleric swooped away, whirling through the circled cross of St. Cuthbert that topped the cathedral's spire, laughing at Jourdain's efforts.

"Can you hurry this up?" Driskoll asked. "I don't know how much longer Mom can hold out."

Kellach swore loud enough for Driskoll's ears to turn red. "It's not working," the apprentice said. "I don't know why! I did everything Mom said. It *should* work!"

Kellach fell to his knees and beat his fists against the obelisk. "Why?" he said. "I am the worst wizard ever!"

Gryphyll clucked his tongue at this. "Why, of course not, my young wizard. You're missing one of the key components to the spell. No one could cast it without that, not even Zendric. That's why he called me here, after all, isn't it?"

Driskoll fought the urge to smack the grin off Gryphyll's face.

"What are you talking about?" Kellach said. "I have all the pieces here. The circle represents the earth. The obelisk stands for the air. The candles around the—" His breath caught in his chest. "Water!" he said. "There's no water."

Gryphyll nodded. "For that, you need a true treasure! A dragon's tear."

"But where are we going to—?" Driskoll stopped himself before he could complete the sentence. "That's what Zendric called you here for?"

Gryphyll grinned and nodded, his eyes wide with delight.

"So," Kellach said, "cry."

He reached into a pocket in his robe to remove an empty metal vial and held it under Gryphyll's face.

"Ah, a treasure . . . ," Gryphyll moaned. It was the saddest Driskoll had ever seen the creature. "I don't think I can."

"You little creep!" Kellach said. "You can't just come here and tell me what we need and then refuse to give it to us. I ought to stomp on your toes until you cry!"

"Don't you dare!" said Moyra. She stepped between Kellach and the little man. Gryphyll peered out around her legs.

"You are so precious, my little wizard," Gryphyll said, smiling wide now, as if Kellach had just told a sly joke. "Imagine: you trying to hurt me. I never could have come up with such a thing."

Kellach clenched his fist and turned away in disgust. He roared at the obelisk again, and then punched it. "Ow, ow, ow!" he said, shaking his injured fist in frustration.

"Please?" Moyra said, getting down on her knees and taking Gryphyll's hands in hers. "Can you cry just a little? For us?"

"I'd love to, my sweet girl," the creature said, a frown almost forming on his lips. "But when I see your face, I just can't." He grinned. "A treasure!"

In the distance, Jourdain let out a shriek.

23

D riskoll reached out and grabbed Gryphyll by the shoulders. The little man had to look up to see Driskoll's eyes. Driskoll didn't know if he could do this. As Kellach's younger brother, he'd gotten used to people ignoring him over the years. But both Kellach and Moyra had tried to get Gryphyll to cry, and they'd failed. There was no one else but Driskoll who could try. And if he failed, they all might die.

"Do you hear that scream, Gryphyll?" Driskoll said. "That's our mother, Jourdain. Lexos is out there with her, hurting her."

Gryphyll frowned for a moment, but then brightened. "Ah, Jourdain? I remember her well as a girl. A treasure! Destined for great things for sure!"

"I never knew her as a girl, only as my mother," Driskoll said. "Then, five years ago, she disappeared. We thought she'd been killed."

The little man looked away for a moment and then grinned.

"But she's not, is she? She's back. Oh, happy day!"

"She'll be dead soon if you don't—" Kellach stalked toward Gryphyll, but Driskoll held up his hand.

"I remember when we first found out Mom was gone," Driskoll continued. "She'd sent us to stay with Moyra and her mother that night, for safety. We sat out most of the battle that nearly destroyed the city right there, staying up all night and playing with Moyra like nothing was going on outside. We ignored the screams and explosions, drowning them out with jokes and laughter, pretending that nothing could hurt us and that we would all live forever.

"Then, sometime around dawn, the noises outside stopped. We heard people cheering outside, and Royma—Moyra's mother—came into the room and unshuttered the windows, letting the light stream in. We smiled then and laughed—real laughs, not the kind we'd been forcing all night long.

"Soon, though, there was a knock at the door. We ignored it. We were too busy cheering the end of the battle. Royma answered it, though.

"When Royma came back into the room, her face was red, and her eyes were puffy. She refused to look at us. I don't think she's looked at Kellach and me the same since.

"Dad came into the room. He was battered and cut. His uniform hung in tatters from his shoulders. The left side of his face was one big bruise, and his arm was in a sling. He limped into that room, and the moment he saw Kellach and me he collapsed to his knees.

"At first, I didn't know what had happened. Everyone had been so happy a moment ago. What could have gone wrong?

"Dad was hurt, sure, but he was alive. That's when it hit me."

"What's that?" Gryphyll said, his little voice raw and low, his lower lip trembling.

Driskoll wiped his own eyes. He'd been crying for a while now and hadn't even noticed. When he spoke, the words stuck in his throat, and he had to choke them out.

"That my mother was gone. That I'd never see her again."

Gryphyll's lower lip stuck out so far from his frown that Driskoll though he might be able to rest his bulbous nose on it. Then, one small, sparkling tear slid down out of his trembling, silver eyes.

Kellach pounced, reaching out with his metal vial to scoop the precious tear from Gryphyll's cheek. Once he had it, the little man threw himself forward into Driskoll's arms and hugged him as tight as he could.

"That," Gryphyll whispered into Driskoll's ear, "is the saddest story I've ever heard." He pushed himself back and grinned at him again, the tear already a fading memory. "Well done, my sweet boy!" he said. "A real treasure!"

Kellach slapped Driskoll on the back and then headed off to complete the spell. The look on his brother's face told Driskoll just how proud he was of him.

"Thank you," Driskoll said to Gryphyll.

"For what, dear boy? You did all the work! You will no doubt be a great bard one day."

Kellach started to chant again. As the young apprentice completed the complex ritual that would do whatever it was that Zendric had intended, a gargantuan demon reared its horned, flaming head above the tops of the tents and stalls in the bazaar and roared.

"We're safe in the circle," Driskoll said. "Right?"

"I'm no wizard," Moyra said, "but I think so. Right, Gryphyll?"

The little man stared up at the demon as it loosed another roar that shook the tents between it and the Great Circle. "Too true," he said. "Too true. Normally."

"What's that supposed to mean?" Driskoll said.

Gryphyll smiled up at him. "My good lad, if your brother succeeds in his efforts—as well we should all hope he does—the Great Circle will be destroyed."

Driskoll gaped at the creature. "Shouldn't we stop him? This is the only thing protecting us from that thing—and all the other demons running through town."

Gryphyll shook his head, then reached up and patted both Driskoll and Moyra on the arm. "Do you think that I wouldn't lend you a hand in a time off need like this," he said. He strode away from them to the edge of the circle and stood between a pair of the burning, miniature obelisks.

Gryphyll spread his arms wide and started to grow. As he did, his skin became thick and covered with wide, silvery scales. Wings stretched out from his back. Long talons grew from his fingers and his toes. Horns sprang from his head, curling back to frame the metallic frill that replaced his hair. The ridge of that flung up high and regal and then ran all the way back along the elongated spine to the very end of the new-formed tail. Within moments, a beautiful silver dragon stood on his haunches, beating his wings, where the little man had once been. He turned and looked over his shoulder at Moyra and Driskoll, grinning just like the little man had.

"I will hold off the demons for as long as I can," the dragon said. His voice was strong and resonant now, but it somehow reminded Driskoll exactly of the little man's nasal tones. "Be safe, my friends!"

With that, the dragon leaped into the sky and flapped its wings in the direction of the giant demon. The beast spotted Gryphyll immediately and produced a blazing club. He waved it at the dragon.

Gryphyll inhaled deep and then let loose a blast of pure cold from inside his icy gut. The demon screeched as the brutal frigidity caressed it, and steam spouted from its skin, obscuring it and the dragon alike.

CHAPTER

24

"A ren't you done yet?" Moyra called back to Kellach.

"Just one more minute," he said. To Driskoll, his brother's voice sounded miles away. Kellach's mind was so wrapped up in concentrating on finishing the spell that Driskoll didn't think anything could stop him.

Then Lexos dropped out of the sky. The cleric landed about a quarter of the way around the Great Circle from where Driskoll and Moyral stood. He didn't fall so much as floated down like a leaf tumbling from a tree.

Driskoll turned to ask Moyra what they should do, but she was already charging toward the cleric. As she ran, she drew her knife and held it in an underhand grip, ready to plunge it into the man.

Lexos landed on his feet but instantly crumbled to his hands and knees. When Moyra reached him, she lashed out with her foot and kicked him onto his back. A moment later, she was on top of him, her knees holding down his arms, her blade at his throat.

"Where's Jourdain?" Moyra demanded.

Lexos tried to buck Moyra off him. Driskoll tackled his legs and held him down.

Moyra repeated her question. As she spoke, she pressed her knife into the man's neck for emphasis.

The cleric laughed in a sick sort of way that made Driskoll guess that he'd broken several ribs. "I don't know," he said, a smarmy smile on his face.

"The truth!" Moyra said, slamming down on the man's chest.

Lexos coughed as if he might try to hack up a lung. He looked like he might have passed out, but he blinked himself back to consciousness. "The last I saw of her, she was falling from the sky," the cleric said. "My guess is she's dead." He glared around Moyra at Driskoll. "For real this time."

Moyra pushed her blade down harder into the cleric's neck. A thin line of crimson rose up along its edge.

"I should kill you," she said, more to herself than to Lexos.

"Go ahead," the cleric said with a sneer. "I have served Erythnul well. He will reward me in this life or the next."

"No," Driskoll said to Moyra, so softly he had to clear his throat to make sure she could hear him. "Don't. He's unarmed. He's hurt. He's no threat to us."

Moyra shuddered so hard that Driskoll could feel it through Lexos's legs. "That's what we all thought the last time—and the time before that." She turned back to glare at him. "Just think of the misery we'd have saved the world if we'd killed him then."

"This is murder, Moyra," Driskoll said. "Don't."

"She won't," Lexos said, grinning up at Moyra. "The girl doesn't have the guts for it. Her father would have slit my throat without a second thought."

"How sure are you about that?" Moyra said, her voice filled with menace. "I stabbed your friend Latislav in the belly just a few hours back."

Lexos smiled patiently. "I'm sure he presented a direct threat to your life at the time. As for myself, I surrender."

Driskoll felt the cleric relax underneath him. Wary of a ruse, though, he kept his hold on the cleric's legs.

"Go ahead, you guttersnipe. Strike. Push your knife through my neck. Revel in my life as it pours out and stains your hands."

Moyra cocked back her hand to deliver a lethal blow. Driskoll felt the cleric tense up in anticipation of his death. The boy thought he heard the man chuckle. At the last second, though, Moyra flipped the knife in her hand and brought down the handle hard against Lexos's temple. The cleric's muscles went slack.

"Move it!" Kellach shouted. Driskoll looked up to see his brother charging straight at him. "We don't want to be here when the spell takes effect."

Driskoll jumped to his feet and pulled Moyra off of Lexos's unconscious form. As she stood, she pointed the tip of her knife at the cleric again, daring him to get up and try to attack her.

Driskoll stepped forward and grabbed Lexos under one of his arms. "Help me!" he said. "We can't leave him here."

Moyra snarled and walked away in disgust. Kellach snatched up Lexos's other arm. Together, the two brothers dragged the cleric after them, out to the edge of the Great Circle.

"Do we have to leave the circle?" Driskoll asked as they deposited Lexos near where Moyra stood, her knife still in her hand.

Kellach shook his head. "This should be good enough—if it works."

The apprentice stared out at the obelisk, a wide smile of anticipation on his face. "This will stun you," he said.

Nothing happened. Driskoll waited a moment longer. Still nothing.

"I'm stunned all right," he said. "I'll admit, I expected something to, well—"

"Happen," Moyra said.

Kellach grimaced, as he chewed on a nail. "Wait," he said. "They've been asleep for a long time. It might take them a bit longer to wake up."

On the steps of Town Hall, a werewolf howled at the silvery moon that hung high and full overhead. As Driskoll snapped his head around to see what had inspired Guffy to be so noisy, he spotted a flight of winged demons heading straight for Main Square. No, not a flight—a flock of flying demons of all shapes and sizes, from quasits to incubi to monsters larger than a house. Their flapping wings blotted out the stars, replacing them only with their evil glowing, red eyes. They shone the same color as the crimson sky of the burning Abyss.

The demons spotted the werewolf, and some of them spun toward him like a flock of birds spying their prey. Most of them, though, dived straight down toward Kellach, Driskoll, and Moyra. The only hope Driskoll had in his heart at that last second was that they might rend the unconscious Lexos to bits too.

Then the slabs of cut stone comprising the interior of the Great Circle started to move. They shuddered at first, breaking loose the cement that had held them together for countless decades. Then they began to buckle upward.

"Hold on!" Kellach shouted. "Here they come!"

The obelisk in the center of the Great Circle began to glow with a white light that seemed to come from deep inside its monolithic stone. As Kellach, Moyra, and Driskoll watched, the light grew brighter and brighter until it became painful to look straight at it. Then a beam of light shot straight out of the top of the obelisk and into the blackness of the sky. It seemed to stretch straight up toward the moon, its light illuminating a wide round globe in the heavens.

The oncoming demons shied away from the light, unwilling to risk being caught in its pure caress. Still, they did not leave. They stayed to watch the scene unfold, almost as if they could not force themselves to look away.

One by one, the stone slabs in the Great Circle—a dozen of them in all—popped up and flipped over to the side, standing straight up on their edges. As they did, something crawled from beneath each one and climbed out into the night air. The scales of the silvery beasts glowed in the light of the burning obelisks. As the creatures rose, they stretched out their wings to sample the fresh air denied to them for so many years during their long hibernation.

"It's full of silver dragons," Driskoll said, his voice strangled with awe.

Kellach laughed. Moyra joined in with him, and soon Driskoll did too. He felt intoxicated with the sight of the majestic creatures as they peered around at their surroundings, each of them glancing down at the people watching for but a moment, before flexing their wings and soaring into the sky.

The first of the dragons burst into the hovering pack of demons and lay about them with fang, wing, and claw. The quasits squeaked in terror and tried to flee, but the dragon caught dozens of them in a blast of icy breath that froze them solid. They rained down from the sky like sack-sized bits of hail.

The other dragons followed the first into the fray, leading with their teeth. The larger demons tried to rally the others to repel the newcomers, but the dragons ripped and tore at them until the demons either fled or fell from the sky.

As the flock of demons dispersed, the dragons pursued them back the way they had come. Blasts of icy coldness brought demon after demon crashing to the earth, and soon the silver dragons ruled the sky for as far as Driskoll could see. When all but one of the dragons had left, winging off toward the West-gate, the last majestic creature turned to Kellach, Moyra, and Driskoll and said, "Well done, young Knights."

Then it flapped upward into the night and flew away.

CHAPTER

25

D riskoll awoke in his own bed to the smell of pancakes. He peeled open his eyes and saw that the bed across the room from his was empty, the blankets thrown to the side.

A smile crept across Driskoll's face as he sat up and stretched. Through the open window, from the streets below, he could hear the sounds of the people of Curston going about their morning business: people chatting, carts rolling, horses clip-clopping down the street. Somewhere, a town crier rang his brassy bell and announced the morning news at the top of his lungs. "Demon invasion repelled!" he shouted. "Curston secure once more!"

Driskoll knew it would be a while before Curston was truly secure again. Besides the open holes that now stood arrayed around the center of the Great Circle, the damage done to the town and the Westgate would take weeks if not months to repair. The fact that the Seal had been remade, though, and the demons destroyed meant a time of unparalleled peace in the city—going back at least as far as Driskoll could remember.

He pulled on a fresh shirt and pants and padded down the stairs to the main floor in his bare feet. Torin, who stood flipping a golden pancake over the stove, turned to give him a wry glare as Driskoll emerged into the room, which occupied most of that level of the house. "A boy helps save a city, and he figures he can sleep all day."

"I think we can give him a break on that," Jourdain said, as she rose from her chair at the dining table, holding up out her arms. "Just this once."

Driskoll savored his mother's embrace for as long as he could. All too soon, she pulled him away so she could look down at him. She still had an inch or two on him.

Jourdain kissed Driskoll on the cheek. "I'm so proud of you," she said. She looked at Kellach. "Of both of you."

"I guess I didn't play any part in this," Torin said in mock jealousy.

Jourdain tossed a kitchen rag at him, and it hit him in the shoulder. "Glory hound," she said with a grin.

Driskoll threw himself into a chair across from Kellach. Jourdain sat between them, with Torin's empty chair across from her.

Driskoll realized that in the five years that Jourdain had been gone they'd always sat in the same spots and left her chair empty—except during those times Moyra joined them for a meal. They'd never said a word to one another about it.

They'd just done it because it felt right. Now Jourdain sat in that once-empty chair, smiling at her husband and sons as she ate a syrup-drenched pancake.

"What are you grinning about?" she said to Driskoll. She reached out to tousle his hair, and he saw that she wore a goofy grin too. None of them seemed to be able to stop smiling.

After the horrors of the night before, it was no wonder that the four of them clung so tightly to their moment of happiness. If life in Curston had taught them anything, it was that life itself was fleeting and precious. They needed to take the moments of joy that came to them and—as Gryphyll might say—treasure them.

Then his thoughts went to the other Knights of the Silver Dragon, the ones he'd only met briefly on the road back from the Dungeons of Doom. They'd spent five years in the Abyss with Jourdain, and just like her they'd come back to fight once more for a town that seemed to barely remember them and their sacrifices.

Before he'd become a knight himself, Driskoll had thought such a role would be filled with fortune and glory. People would recognize the risks that he and his fellows had taken for them, and they would shower him and the other Knights with gifts and respect—even adoration. He'd long since lost those illusions.

You didn't become a knight to gain things. Knights *did* things. They fought evil, righted wrongs, and saved people because they knew it was the right thing to do—the only thing for good people to do. You didn't need to be a knight to do those things, of course. You just had to answer the call when it came, to lend a hand when it was needed. Being a part of an order of knights just meant you had friends you could call on to help you too. It was like being part of a family.

As Driskoll basked in the glow of the reunification of his blood family, he wondered about the fate of his extended families: the other Knights, the watchers who served under his father, the people with whom he shared the streets of Curston. Despite the way he knew it would shatter the good mood running through his home, he had to know.

"What news do we have?" Driskoll asked.

Torin grimaced as he took his place at the table with the others. "We lost a good number of watchers, some of our best. I won't know the final numbers until later today, but my guess is we suffered at least fifty percent casualties, maybe more."

Driskoll's heart fell: over half of the watch gone. He'd seen the demons they'd fought so valiantly against. He knew what kind of damage they could do. The numbers shouldn't have shocked him so much, but they did.

"Guffy?"

"You mean Sergeant Dogface?" Torin asked with a smile. "He's fine. Better than ever. It seems transforming into a werewolf agrees with him."

Torin used his fork to stab a piece of pancake off of Driskoll's plate and plot it into his mouth. "Keep that little tidbit of information to yourself if you can," he said to Driskoll. "He'd rather not have every monster hunter that strolls through town looking for him."

"What about Gwinton?"

Torin turned grim once more and reached across the table to hold Jourdain's hand. "He lives, although he mourns Lettie. He missed her every day she was gone. To have her get so close to coming home but to be killed on the city's doorstep . . . "

"Kaisle came through just fine," Jourdain said, eager to move on to other subjects. "He and Grax spent most of the battle counting kills against each other. I understand they gathered some amazing trophies as well."

Torin nodded. "Kruncher and Carluzzi did a fine job as magical support. Without their help, the watchers would have lost scores more. I understand Kruncher wants to talk with you two."

Driskoll's breakfast turned to ice in his stomach. After all, he and Driskoll had fought with Kruncher's son, Kruncher, the day the half-orc bully had been killed—by Lexos. "Why?" he said around a mouthful of pancake.

"To thank you," Jourdain said. "He's embarrassed by how badly his son behaved while he was gone. The poor child was left without a mother or a father after the first Sundering. It's no wonder he fell in with the wrong crowd."

"He's grateful that you helped bring Lexos to justice for his son's murder, though," Torin said.

"I can't believe Lexos actually surrendered." Driskoll shook his head.

"Lexos is smart enough to know when he's been beaten." Torin grinned. "And your mother gave him the beating of his life."

Jourdain shrugged. "He did fight hard. I'll give him that. But I have had years to dream of the spells I'd use if I ever had a chance to battle him. He didn't have much left after I was done with him." Jourdain laughed. "If I do say so myself."

Kellach looked up at his father. "Do you think it's safe to leave him in jail? I mean, last time we imprisoned him, he found a way to escape. You're sure this isn't another one of his tricks?"

"Breddo himself made sure that Lexos's cell is secure this time—and that no one feels inclined to help set him free," said Jourdain.

"No one knows the jail better than Breddo," said Torin, "inside and out."

"Hey," a voice called from the front of the house, "I resemble that accusation."

"Breddo!" Jourdain said. She leaped to her feet to throw open the door, revealing Moyra and her parents standing there. "Come on in!" she said. "All of you!"

Jourdain hugged each of them as they came in: first Moyra, then Royma, and Breddo last of all. With each one, her smile grew wider and wider. "It's so good to see you all together again."

Kellach and Driskoll got up to share an embrace with Moyra. She looked happier than he could ever remember seeing her.

Royma seemed almost drunk with joy. She'd been so sour and fearful ever since the Sundering of the Seal. To see her like this stunned Driskoll.

"So," Breddo said, "I see you've already eaten, but we wondered if we might invite our good friends here out for a stroll through the town?"

"To tour the destruction?" Torin said. Being the captain of the watch and Breddo renowned as the greatest thief in town, the two men often butted heads over issues far weightier than a midmorning stroll.

Breddo winced, but with a smile. "It's true that Curston has seen better days, but I don't think I've ever been more hopeful about its future. Just look at how far we came after the Sundering of the Seal."

"You think the city can bounce back that quickly again?" Jourdain asked.

Breddo nodded. "Where Torin here sees destruction and despair, I see opportunity and hope. It's not often that a city this tough and hardened gets a chance to start over again."

The thief put his arm around his wife and daughter. Moyra grinned up at him. "I know this city as well as anyone—even you, Torin," Breddo said. "And I have no doubt that we'll recover from this, thrive even. Without the nightly attacks from creatures wiggling out of the Dungeons of Doom, just think about what we can do. I'm thinking about asking the town council to rename the place Promise again."

"Why not?" said Kellach, standing up to leave on the walk

Breddo had proposed. Jourdain rose next to him.

"I think it's a great idea," Moyra said. "But then, I did suggest it."

"Promise," Driskoll said, as he joined them. "I like the sound of that."

The six of them looked over at Torin, who still sat at the table. He looked at them all, then dropped his fork and got to his feet. "All right," he said to them, a rare grin stretched across his rugged face. "If the Knights of the Silver Dragon are willing to give it a try, who am I to say no?"

🐾 🐾 🐾 🐾 🐾

Later that day, Kellach led Moyra and Driskoll through Curston's shattered streets to Zendric's tower. The city still stank of brimstone, and tendrils of smoke rose from extinguished fires in every direction, but the sun shone down through a clear blue sky, and anything seemed possible again.

"Did Mom say what she wanted?" Driskoll asked.

Kellach didn't glance back as he threaded his way through the crowded streets. "She mentioned cleaning up the tower and inventorying everything. With Zendric gone, she's the most powerful wizard in town now. She'll need to go through his notes and figure out everything she's missed in the past five years. It's a lot of responsibility."

Moyra wrinkled her nose. "She probably just wants a hand with a broom or three. There are corners in that place that haven't been cleaned in a hundred years."

All three of the friends laughed at that. When they turned a corner and the tower swung into view, though, they fell silent. The sight of the tower hammered home the fact that Zendric had disappeared from their lives, possibly forever.

"He'll be all right," Driskoll said, trying to hold out some hope. "Won't he?"

"Your mother survived in the Abyss for all that time," said Moyra.

"But she had a bunch of friends to help her out," Kellach said. "He's all alone."

"Do you think he's . . . dead?" said Driskoll. The thought made him shiver. Having only glimpsed that horrible realm, he didn't see how anyone could survive in it for long.

Kellach shook his head, perhaps too emphatically. "If anyone could live in the Abyss, it would be Zendric." He put a hand on Driskoll's shoulder as they reached the tower's entrance, which stood wide open. "Someday he'll come stamping out of that door toward us, just like nothing had ever happened."

Driskoll summoned up a wry grin, hoping his brother was right.

"Come in, you three!" Jourdain's voice rang out from somewhere inside the tower. "I have something to show you."

Driskoll's smile turned real as he pushed past the others and raced into the tower. Inside, he could see that Jourdain had made some progress cleaning up the mess. Most everything had been put neatly back into its place, no doubt by magical means.

The spiritkeeper, though, no longer stood on the mantel.

Instead, it rested in the center of the main table, its smoky interior pulsing with a reddish glow. Driskoll stopped and stared at the mystical device for a moment. His mother's voice distracted him before he could ponder it for too long though.

"I'm upstairs!" Jourdain called.

This time, Kellach led the trio up the stairs, with Moyra on his tail and Driskoll bringing up the rear. When they reached the next floor—Zendric's workplace—they saw Jourdain sitting at Zendric's desk. She put down an inked quill she held in her hand and smiled at them.

"I'm so glad you're here," she said. "I have the most wonderful thing to show you."

Driskoll shot Kellach a quizzical look, but Kellach only shrugged.

Jourdain strolled over to the far side of the chamber, where a long tapestry hung down the length of the wall. It depicted scenes from the history of Curston, starting with the founding, right up next to the ceiling and ending with what looked like an image of a dozen silver dragons battling a horde of demons.

"I know about this," Kellach said, a hint of disappointment in his voice. "It magically embroiders itself with the latest of the city's legends."

"Hey!" Moyra said. "We're on here!"

Driskoll peered at the tapestry and spotted indications of their adventures: a spiritkeeper here, a clockwork dragonet there—even all three of their faces. "That's immortality for you," he said in an awed voice. "Thanks, Mom."

Jourdain grinned. "That is amazing, of course, and I couldn't be prouder. However, it's not the reason I called you here."

Jourdain pulled the tapestry aside, revealing a tall, oval mirror beneath. The glass formed a flawless reflection, and as Driskoll stared at it, he smiled to see his mother, his brother, and his best friend encircled in the worn, wooden frame. Then Jourdain tucked the tapestry behind a hook along the wall and reached out to tap the surface of the mirror in a pattern that Driskoll could not follow. When she stepped back from it, the image twisted and warped for a moment, then became blacker than the darkest night. Driskoll could have sworn he heard someone screaming, although the sound seemed muffled and distant.

"Zendric?" Jourdain said, her voice soft and expectant.

A light blazed somewhere behind the mirror's frame, illuminating the area beyond it, as if the mirror had somehow become a window instead. Images spun about in the frame, and Driskoll had to blink to prevent feeling dizzy. When he looked again, he saw Zendric's face smiling back at him through the mirror. It stretched taller and wider than what was possible, but Driskoll realized that this was an image he saw, not the real thing, and it had been magnified as if he was peering through one of those strange lenses held on a series of armatures in Zendric's laboratory. Then the image spoke.

"Hello, my Knights," Zendric said. "I'm pleased to know you are doing so well. Jourdain had told me as much, but I wanted to see you with my own eyes."

"How?" Driskoll said, his eyes wide with wonder. He had

dozens more questions to ask, but he couldn't manage to get more than that one word out.

"Your mother." Zendric seemed to lock eyes with Jourdain. "As I was moving through the Seal at the last moment she tossed me this small mirror. It is magically linked to the larger mirror in my study—as you can see."

"So you're not dead!" Driskoll said.

"Hardly." Zendric gave the boy a warm smile, which faded fast. "At least not for now. As your mother can tell you, every day in the Abyss is a challenge to survive."

"I will guide you through it as best I can," Jourdain said. "And together we will find a way to bring you back."

"Can't you do that now?" Moyra asked. "Just walk through the mirror, or something?"

"It's not quite that simple," Zendric said, his eyes sparkling at the girl. "To come home, it seems I would have to leave open a door behind me, one that any of the demons could use to follow me to Curston. That is not acceptable."

"But there has to be a way," Driskoll said.

"I believe there is," Jourdain said, putting a hand on her son's shoulder. "I don't yet know what it is, but we will find it—sooner than later."

"Until then, my good Knights," Zendric said, "I leave our fair city in the hands of Jourdain and you. I can think of no better guardians."

The wizard glanced away then. "It is not safe for me to speak with you long. I must go. But know this." He stared directly at them now. "I will always be here for you. When you need me, call upon me, and I will do all that I can. Farewell!"

With that, the image in the mirror spun around again and turned black. A moment later, the mirror's surface shimmered and became reflective again. Jourdain unhooked the tapestry and let it fall over the mirror once more.

Driskoll reached out and took his mother's hand. "Will he be all right?" he asked.

Jourdain grimaced. "I wish I knew. He can take care of himself better than anyone else I know, your father included."

She gathered both of her boys into her arms. "When Zendric first disappeared through that gate, I would have given anything to trade places with him. Now, though," she looked down at them, "I don't see how I could ever give up being your mother again."

"You never did, Mom," Kellach said. "We always knew you'd come back."

"Just like we know Zendric will too," Moyra said.

Driskoll allowed himself a soft smile. "Until then, we'll be sure to take great care of this town. What else would you expect of the Knights of the Silver Dragon?"

ACKNOWLEDGMENTS

Special thanks to Nina Hess,
Emily Fiegenschuh, and Peter Archer.

This isn't the first time Gryphyll has stepped in to lend the Knights of the Silver Dragon a hand. Check out their very first adventure with Gryphyll in . . .

THE HIDDEN DRAGON
KNIGHTS OF THE SILVER DRAGON, BOOK 7
ISBN 0-7869-3748-3

When Moyra's mother is arrested for stealing a medallion, Kellach, Moyra, and Driskoll set out to clear her name. They must find the necklace's maker: a silver dragon who lives somewhere in the mountains outside Curston. But the mountains are filled with dangerous creatures. And not far behind, an old enemy watches, determined to stop the Knights at any cost. Will the Knights make it to the dragon's lair alive?

Available in bookstores now! If you don't see it on the shelf, be sure to ask one of the salespeople to order it.

**Want a sneak peek of *The Hidden Dragon* right now?
Start reading . . .**

Moyra paced the small space of the underground room. Driskoll sat on the floor and leaned against a wall, watching her.

The single candle burned in its holder, which they'd placed in the middle of the floor. The candlelight threw eerie shadows across the dirt walls of the pit. The shadows loomed and danced as the candle flickered, making Driskoll think of ghosts and other strange things that lurked in dark corners.

Driskoll wasn't sure, but he didn't think much time had passed since they'd heard the door shut and they knew they were trapped.

In a hole.

In Lexos's home.

If the situation weren't so serious, Driskoll might have laughed at how absurd it all was.

"And to think that just a few days ago, I was complaining how bored I was," Driskoll said.

"You find this exciting?" Moyra shot back.

"If you mean sitting in a hole in the ground, no, this is not exciting."

"Then what do you mean?" she said as she reached one wall and began to walk to the other.

"I don't know. But I do know that you'll figure some way out of here."

Moyra snorted. "Like what! We've already tried everything!"

They'd stood on the wooden ladder that led into the hole, and had tried to raise the wooden door. But the bolt was too strong. They'd considered burning the door with the candle, but then they'd realized that the ceiling, including the door, was covered by a sheet of iron. Dig their way out? They'd scratched for a few moments, only to find that the dirt was more clay than loose soil. All they'd gotten for their efforts was tons of dirt under their fingernails and muddy knees.

"If only I had my tools!" Moyra absently traced a circle on the dirt floor with her foot.

"If I had my sword, we could chop our way out," Driskoll added.

"Well, you don't have your sword and I don't have my tools," Moyra said. She screeched in frustration. "You know, I don't even care what Lexos does with us when he comes back. I only care about what's happening right now. And the fact that I don't know is driving me nuts!" She glared up at the trapdoor and shook her fist.

"Moyra, what are you doing?" Driskoll asked.

"I'm putting a curse on old Lexos, that's—" She suddenly stopped and cocked her ear toward the door "Did you hear that?"

Driskoll shook his head. "I didn't hear anything.

Moyra held up a hand. "Shh! There! There it is again!"

Driskoll stretched his legs and stood. He heard it, too. "That scratching noise? It's probably just a mouse or something."

"Great," Moyra said. "Just great. Now we have rats to keep us company."

"I said mouse, not rat."

Moyra rolled her eyes. "Oh, that makes me feel so much better." She walked up the ladder and waited.

"What are you doing now?"

"Shh!" She held her fist below the door, waiting, waiting—then she pounded as loudly as she could.

"What did you do that for?" Driskoll asked, peering up at her.

"To scare away the rat, of course."

"Rat?" said a voice on the other side of the door. "I beg your pardon. I may be small, but I am no rat!"

Moyra was so surprised, she nearly fell off the ladder. She climbed down quickly and stood next to Driskoll. They both peered at the door above them.

"Hello? Are you still down there?" the voice spoke again.

"We weren't imagining it," Driskoll whispered. "There really *is* someone there."

"Well, let's not stand around with our mouths open," Moyra said. "Yes!" she shouted. "We're here! Below the door!"

"Why, you are, aren't you?" the voice said.

Driskoll didn't stop to think who the voice belonged to. The voice meant freedom. The voice meant escape. "Can you lift the door?" he hollered up. "I think it might be heavy!"

"Heavy, you say?" They heard a few scurries, then a squeaky noise, like metal rubbing against metal. "Bit of a bolt, you see," the voice said. "Now, let's see if this door is, indeed, heavy."

Driskoll watched, astonished, as the door inched its way upward.

"A little help would be nice," the voice said.

"Dumb!" Driskoll said. Both he and Moyra fought for position on the ladder. They both thrust their hands against the door, and with the aid of their mysterious helper, the door flew back effortlessly. Moyra bounded up the ladder first, with Driskoll a close second. They didn't give a moment's thought to the candle still burning on the dirt floor.

Scanning the room, Moyra wrinkled her forehead. "I don't see anyone."

"He must be here somewhere." Driskoll looked quickly around the room. The trapdoor he and Moyra had flung upward now lay open on the floor, revealing the pit below. Mystified, he called out. "Hello? Rat-person? Where are you?"

"The door that you thought might be heavy? Well, it is rather heavy when it is lying across one's person."

"Oh, my goodness!" Moyra exclaimed, pointing at the trapdoor. Driskoll's gaze followed her finger and beneath the slab of wood, he saw two wiggling feet. Driskoll ran around to the other side of the pit, hoisted up the door, and let it drop shut with a thud.

"Thank you so much!" Driskoll said. "We have something

urgent we have to do, and . . . " Driskoll's words trailed off. He watched as the most grotesque being he'd ever seen wobbled to his feet, then began brushing himself off.

The creature looked a bit like a dwarf, but not quite as big or as broad. His tall, rounded ears stuck out from the sides of his head, and his queer nose hung, long and bulbous. He wore short trousers that revealed hairy legs, and boots that were ankle-high and had pointy toes. A loose tunic with a wide belt completed his attire.

Momentarily startled, Moyra managed to ask, "And who do we have the pleasure of thanking?"

"Pleased to meet you, too." The grotesque creature smiled and his face crinkled, like a piece of old parchment. "I am Gryphyll!"

Moyra bowed. "I'm Moyra, and this is Driskoll."

"A treasure! A treasure!" said the little fellow.

"Don't you mean 'pleasure'?" Driskoll said, shaking his hand. The chubby little fingers wrapped around two of Driskoll's own. Driskoll expected the hand to feel moist and slimy, like that of a toad or a fish. Instead, the little fingers were quite strong.

"Nope, treasure, treasure it is!" The face crinkled even more.

Driskoll looked about Lexos's hut. It suddenly dawned on him that anyone with a connection to Lexos should probably not be trusted, no matter if he had saved their lives. "Um, I don't mean to be rude or ungrateful, but what are you doing here?"

"Why, I live here!" Gryphyll said.

"You live here?" Moyra asked. "I thought Lexos lived here."

"Yes, Lexos. Not a very nice man, is he? Seemed to think the hut was empty, and just walked right in." The little creature hobbled away from the door and across the room. "Never bothered to look around, he didn't, and only lit a few candles. It's very easy for me to hide in the shadows, don't you know."

Driskoll nodded. "We can see that." He studied the fellow closely. "What are you, Gryphyll? Half dwarf?"

"What am I?" the creature asked, perplexed. "Why, I'm Gryphyll!"

"Yes, but you see . . ." Driskoll pointed to himself. "I'm a human. It's not who I am, it's what I am."

The creature shook his head. "I'm Gryphyll, that's all I know."

"Whatever," Driskoll said abruptly. "This has been really fun, but we must be going. We have important matters to see to."

"Yes, nasty business, that. I heard your conversation with Lexos. He has your mother, has he?"

"In a way," Moyra said. As she spoke, she re-bolted the door and kicked dirt across it so Lexos wouldn't realize right away that they had escaped. "It's a long story."

"Something about a medallion, too, if I heard right."

"Yes, you heard right." Driskoll spied their gear in the corner where Lexos had tossed it. He handed Moyra her things, then buckled his sword back around his waist. "Look, whatever you are, we hate to be rescued and run, but we really have to go," Driskoll said. "We have to find my brother and Lexos and make sure Moyra's mother is all right."

"I completely understand," said the accommodating little fellow. He stood there with his hands folded in front of him, his small purple eyes twinkling up at Moyra.

A silly smile came over Moyra's face. "Driskoll, I think we should take him with us."

Gryphyll beamed.

"What!" Driskoll shook his head. "No! Absolutely not."

"We can't leave him here," she insisted. "Who knows what Lexos will do to him after he discovers we're gone."

"Moyra, we don't even know who he is or what he is. He could be working for Lexos for all we know."

Moyra waved that away. "Doubtful." She turned to Gryphyll. "Look, we have to move quickly, but do you want to come with us?"

Gryphyll smile grew brighter, revealing a few teeth, and a few spaces where teeth might once have been. "Quite kind of you, miss!" He looked up at Driskoll. "But does the young sir wish my company too?"

Driskoll rolled his eyes and glanced at Moyra. "Oh, all right. I don't exactly like this, but I know you. You won't let it rest, and we'll spend the next ten minutes arguing about it." Driskoll turned to Gryphyll. "Come on then. We have to hurry."

Gryphyll waddled over and took both Moyra and Driskoll's hands, smiling all the while. He looked as if he wanted to swing between them, like a child on a sunny afternoon at the park. "Don't worry, sir. I'm swifter on my feet than you'd believe."

"I hope so," Driskoll said. "Because suddenly I feel like we're running out of time."

Want to read more? As for
The Hidden Dragon
at your local bookstore!

THE NEW ADVENTURES

THE TRINISTYR TRILOGY

The Trinistyr
Ancient holy relic
Cursed symbol of power
Key to Nearra's future . . . or her destruction

WIZARD'S CURSE

Christina Woods

Imbued with vestiges of Asvoria's power, Nearra is convinced
she can restore her magical heritage. Will Nearra find
the strength to break the wizard's curse?
September 2005

WIZARD'S BETRAYAL

Jeff Sampson

Betrayals come to light. New powers arise. And a startling
revelation threatens to destroy Nearra, once and for all.
January 2006

WIZARD'S RETURN

Dan Willis

Can the companions stand together and fight the final battle
for Nearra and Jirah's future?
May 2006

Ask for **Dragonlance: The New Adventures** books at your favorite bookstore!

For more information visit www.mirrorstonebooks.com

For ages ten and up.

THE NEW ADVENTURES

A Practical Guide to Dragons
By Sindri Suncatcher

Sindri Suncatcher—wizard's apprentice—opens up
his personal notebooks to share his knowledge of these
awe-inspiring creatures, from the life cycle of a kind copper
dragon to the best way to counteract a red dragon's fiery
breath. This lavishly illustrated guide showcases the wide
array of fantastic dragons encountered on the world of Krynn.

The perfect companion to the Dragonlance: The New
Adventures series, for both loyal fans and new readers alike.

Sindri Suncatcher is a three-and-a-half foot tall kender,
who enjoys storytelling, collecting magical tokens, and
fighting dragons. He lives in Solamnia and is currently
studying magic under the auspices of the black-robed
wizard Maddoc. You can catch Sindri in the midst of
his latest adventure in *The Wayward Wizard*.

For more information visit www.mirrorstonebooks.com

For ages ten and up.

CHALLENGE MONSTERS

BE THE HERO

BATTLE YOUR FRIENDS

If you like adventures and challenges
you'll love the D&D® Miniatures Game.

Play out furious battles with your friends
or collect and trade the figures.

Ask for the D&D Miniatures Entry Pack
at your favorite book or game store and get ready to battle!

For more information visit **www.wizards.com**

THE NEW ADVENTURES

Want to know more about the Dragonlance world?

Want to know how it all began?

A RUMOR OF DRAGONS
Volume 1

NIGHT OF THE DRAGONS
Volume 2

THE NIGHTMARE LANDS
Volume 3

TO THE GATES OF PALANTHAS
Volume 4

HOPE'S FLAME
Volume 5

A DAWN OF DRAGONS
Volume 6

By Margaret Weis & Tracy Hickman

For more information visit www.mirrorstonebooks.com

For ages ten and up.
Gift Sets Available